THE USBORNE B[OOK OF]

the internet

Philippa Wingate and Mark Wallace

Designed and illustrated by Andy Griffin,
Isaac Quaye and Zöe Wray

Technical consultants: Nick Bell and
Nigel Williams, Director of Childnet International

Additional consultancy by Thom[...]
Michael Sullivan and Liam[...]

Managing editor: Jane C[...]
Managing designers: Mary Cartwright and Stephen[...]

Additional illustrations by John[...]
Cover design by Russel[...]

About this section of the book

The Internet, also known as "the Net", can seem like a huge and confusing place. Every day you'll hear people talking about it, using jargon, buzzwords and technobabble.

Don't panic. As new software is developed and better techniques for exploring the Internet are introduced, it's becoming an easier place to find your way around. This book will make it even easier.

Net knowledge

This section of the book introduces you to the Net. It tells you what it is, how it works and describes all the fun and interesting things you can find on it.

This section includes information on how to go "online" yourself, which means getting connected to the Net. It details what equipment and software you will need, and how to find a company that will give you access to the Net.

All the main facilities the Net offers are introduced, and there is advice on how to use the programs that help you to explore them.

Getting help

On pages 38 and 39, there's a section covering some of the problems you may come across when using the Net. It explains what may be causing them and how to deal with them.

There are lots of new words connected with the Net. To help you, there's a glossary for quick reference on pages 43 to 45. Use the index on page 111 to find out where you can read fuller explanations of unfamiliar words. There's even a list of Internet slang on page 46.

Interesting things

On pages 41 and 42 there is a selection of some of the interesting things you will find on the Net.

The Internet and its technology are changing rapidly. Information about it goes out of date quickly. Some things on the Net change or disappear, so it's difficult to guarantee that all the references in this book will remain correct. There is, however, lots of basic information that will be invaluable to a new user.

Netscape Navigator

There are many different Internet software packages available. *Netscape Navigator*® is a popular program for exploring the Net. It is used for most of the examples in this section of the book.

If you have a computer already set up to use the Internet, you may have different software installed or you may have a different version of *Netscape*. Don't worry. Internet programs are often very similar. Using the examples in this book as a guide, you will be able to figure out how to use your own programs, even if some of their buttons and menu items have slightly different names.

Alternatively, on page 42, you can find out where to get your own copy of the *Netscape Navigator* program.

Netscape Navigator *is a popular program used to explore the Net.*

What is the Internet?

The Internet is a vast computer network linking together millions of smaller networks all over the world.

On these pages you can find out exactly what a network is and how the computers on the Internet are connected to one another.

What is a network?

A network is the name given to a group of computers and computer equipment that have been joined together so they can share information and resources. The computers in an office, for example, are often networked so that they can use the same files and printers.

All the computers linked to the Internet can exchange information with each other. It's as easy to communicate with a computer on the other side of the world as with one that is right next door.

Once your own computer is connected to the Net it is like a spider in the middle of a huge web. All the threads of the web can bring you information from other computers.

Servers and clients

There are two main types of computers on the Internet. The ones which store, sort and distribute information are called hosts, or servers. Those that access and use this information, such as your computer at home, are called clients. A server computer serves a client computer, like a store owner helping a customer.

The picture below shows how the computer networks in different organizations in a town are linked together by the Net.

People can connect their computers at home to the Net.

At school, children can use the Net to learn and communicate with children in other countries.

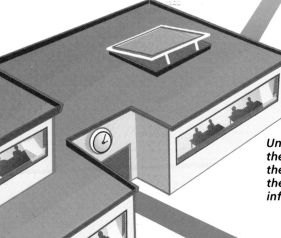

Universities all over the world can use the Net to share their research information.

Cables link one computer network to another.

People can use the computers at this special café to access the Net.

Sometimes satellite links are used to link networks.

Telephone lines

The computer networks that make up the Net are linked together by private and public telephone systems. They can send and receive information along telephone lines. These lines range from cables made of twisted copper wires, to cables containing glass strands, that can carry lots of data at high speeds (over a thousand times faster than copper phone lines). Some networks can be linked by radio waves and microwaves. Networks in different countries and continents are often joined by undersea cables or by satellites.

Cables can run under seas and oceans.

The largest computers on the Net are connected by links known as backbones.

Connections

Some computers, especially ones used in large organizations such as universities, government departments and big businesses, have a "dedicated" Net connection. This means that they are linked to the Net all the time.

People using computers in homes and offices usually don't have dedicated connections. They can join or "hook up" to the Net by using the telephone to dial up a connection with a computer that is already online.

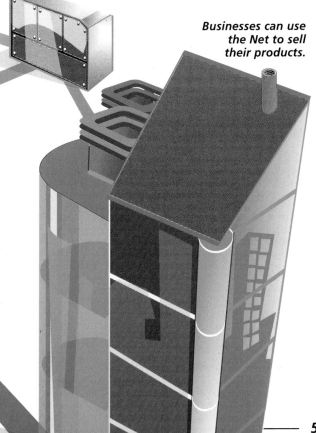

This computer belongs to a company that provides people at home or in offices with Net access.

Businesses can use the Net to sell their products.

🌐 How big?

From huge supercomputers to small personal computers, all kinds of computers make up the Net. There are already tens of millions of host computers, and every month three million new hosts and almost 50,000 networks are added to it. These figures are increasing rapidly.

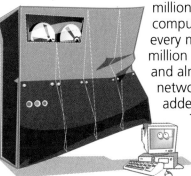

What's on the Net?

From games to gossip, messages to music, and shopping to academic research, once you have access to the Internet, you can do a huge variety of things. These pages show you just some of them.

Information

There are many computers on the Net storing millions of files of information which are free for you to use. There are cartoons, art galleries, magazines and information which could help you with your work or hobbies.

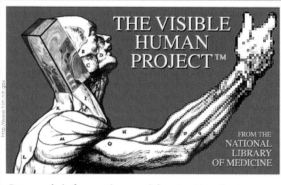

Send messages.

Read a selection of cartoons.

Research information and fascinating facts.

Listen to music or news on Internet radio.

Communicate by Internet telephone.

Join in guided tours around museums and monuments.

Communication

There are millions of Net users all over the world with whom you can communicate, for work or for pleasure. You can send messages, chat, or take part in debates and discussions with other people who share your interests.

Look at beautiful pictures and photographs.

Services

Some computers on the Net provide you with services. You can use them to order flowers, get financial advice, find out train or airline times, book tickets for a show, check the weather report and catch some up-to-date news.

Play a wide selection of games.

Use a video telephone.

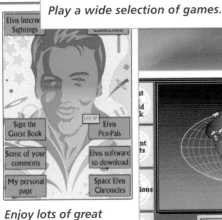
Enjoy lots of great music and fan clubs.

Find things just for kids.

Get a variety of financial information.

Check train timetables and ticket prices.

Look at up-to-date weather forecasts.

Programs

There are lots of programs available for you to copy onto your computer. Some are free to use; others you'll need to pay for. There are programs for playing games, listening to music or watching videos, as well as the latest programs to help you use the Net more efficiently.

Surfing in cyberspace

Cyberspace is the name given to the imaginary space you travel in when you use the Net. Even though you stay in one place, you make an imaginary journey around the world by linking up to computers in different places. Moving around the Net is also known as "surfing".

How does the Net work?

Before two computers on the Internet can exchange information, they need to be able to find each other and communicate in a language that they can both understand.

Name and number

To enable computers on the Net to locate each other, they have unique addresses, called Internet Protocol (IP) addresses. IP addresses take the form of numbers. Numbers are difficult to remember, so each computer is also given a name, known as its domain name. The name has three main sections that give information about where the computer is located. Each section is separated by a dot.
  Here's an imaginary domain name:

usborne.co.uk *This name tells you what organization the user works in.*

usborne.co.uk *This identifies the type of organization.*

usborne.co.uk *This tells you the geographical location or country.*

Country codes

Many countries have their own code. Here are some you may come across:

au Australia
ca Canada
de Germany
fr France
nl Netherlands
se Sweden
uk United Kingdom

If an address has no country code, this usually indicates that a computer is in the USA.

Organizations

Here's a list of some of the codes for the types of organizations found in domain names:

ac   an academic organization
co or **com** a commercial organization
edu   an educational institution
gov   a government body
net   an organization involved in running the Net
org   a non profit-making organization

Computer talk

To make sure that all the computers on the Net can communicate with each other, they all use the same language. It is called TCP/IP (Transmission Control Protocol/Internet Protocol).
  TCP/IP ensures that when data is sent from one computer to another, it is transmitted in a particular way and that it arrives safely in the right place. If, for example, one computer sends a picture to another computer, the picture is broken down into small "packets" of data. Each packet includes information about where it has come from and where it is going to. The packets travel via the Net to the destination computer where they are reassembled.

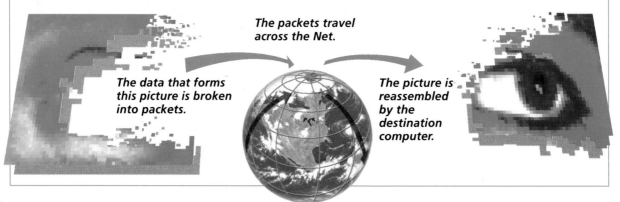

The packets travel across the Net.

The data that forms this picture is broken into packets.

The picture is reassembled by the destination computer.

Here's a brief history of how the Net began and how it became the worldwide network that it is today.

1960s The US Defense Department launched a project to design a computer network that could withstand nuclear attack. If part of the network was destroyed, information could be transmitted to its destination by alternative routes. The network became known as ARPANET (Advanced Research Projects Agency NETwork).

1970s Supercomputers in universities and companies throughout America were linked so that they could share research information.

1980s A new network called NSFNET (National Science Foundation NETwork) was set up.

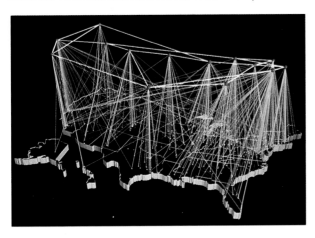

This diagram shows the main connections on the NSFNET on a map of the USA.

NSFNET was a network exchanging non-commercial information.

1990s The network was opened up to everyone, including commercial companies and people using computers at home. The World Wide Web (see page 15) made the Net easier to use and, as a result, it expanded rapidly.

Who controls the Net?

Despite constant attempts by many governments and large organizations, nobody actually controls the Net. It is made up of lots of individual networks which are owned by somebody, but nobody owns all of it.

A test run on the Net

Now that you know the basics of what the Internet is and how it works, you should try it out.

You may find you belong to an organization that is already online. Many schools, colleges and universities have networks linked to the Net. Alternatively, you may work in an office that has computers online.

If you can't gain access in this way, ask a friend who is online to give you a demonstration.

You might find a local museum or library has Net access. Some bookstores and computer stores have computers on which you can explore the Net.

Another good way of trying out the Net is to go to a cybercafé. These are special cafés where you can pay to use computers that are connected to the Net.

This cybercafé is located in the Centre Georges Pompidou, in Paris.

Essential equipment

Whether you want to get connected to the Internet at school, at work or at home, you will need three essential pieces of equipment: a computer, a modem, and a telephone line. You will also need a selection of Internet software.

A computer

It is possible to connect to the Net with almost any computer. However, to make the most of all the facilities the Net offers, you will need at least a 486 DX33 IBM compatible PC, or a Macintosh 68030 series, or an Atari or Amiga computer of the equivalent power.

Your computer needs at least 8MB of RAM. RAM is part of your computer's memory. It is measured in bytes. A megabyte (MB) is just over a million bytes.

Special Net computers

Besides ordinary computers, there are two devices specifically designed for using the Net: network computers and set-top boxes.

Network computers are computers that can only be used to access the Net. They connect up to larger computers on the Net and use them to store and process data. They are different from ordinary computers, because they can operate with a smaller hard disk, which is the part of a computer where data is stored. They also need less memory, which is where data is processed. This makes network computers cheaper than normal computers.

A set-top box

Set-top boxes are devices that can be connected to a television. They allow you to access the Net, with your television's screen acting as a monitor. Set-top boxes are also cheaper to buy than ordinary computers.

A modem

To go online, you will need a modem. This is a device that enables computers to communicate with each other via telephone lines.

A modem converts the data produced by a computer into a form that can be sent along telephone lines. That data is received by a computer that is connected to the Net. It is then routed via the Net to its destination. The picture below shows two computers exchanging data.

1. This computer produces data in the form of electric pulses.

2. This modem converts the data into a form that can travel along telephone lines.

3. The data is received by a computer on the Net and routed to its destination.

4. Another modem converts the data back into electric pulses.

5. The destination computer receives and processes the electric pulses.

Which modem?

You can buy three main types of modems: desktop modems, internal modems which fit inside your computer, and PCMCIA modems which are used with small, notebook computers.

Whichever modem you choose, make sure that it works with your kind of computer and that you have a telephone point near your computer that you can plug it into.

A PCMCIA modem is the size of a credit card.

Modem speed

When you buy a modem it is important to consider how fast it works. The speed at which modems transfer data to and from the Net is measured in bits per second (bps).

When using the Internet, it is a good idea to use a modem which operates at a speed of at least 33,600 bps. These modems are becoming increasingly cheap to buy.

When you dial up a connection to the Net, it's just like making an ordinary telephone call. A high speed modem reduces the amount of time you need to be on the phone, and that can save money.

Serial ports

An external modem plugs into your computer via a socket called a serial port. If you buy an external modem, you will need a high speed serial port to handle the speed at which data is being transferred.

Most modern computers will have high speed serial ports, but check your computer manual. If your computer doesn't have one, you can add one by buying a device called an expansion card.

Extras

Expansion cards are printed circuit boards which slot inside your computer to enable it to perform particular functions. For example, if you want to use the Net to listen to music, you'll need a sound card and speakers attached to your computer. If you want to watch video clips, consider buying a special graphics card to improve their appearance.

Expansion cards

Internet software

Most of the companies that provide you with a connection to the Net (see page 12) will supply all the software you need as part of their service. They will send you disks or a CD containing Internet software that is compatible with your computer and modem.

The software provided will usually include a dialer program to operate your modem and enable your computer to connect to the Net. There will be software that enables your computer to communicate with all the other computers on the Net. You should also be provided with a collection of programs that allows you to do things such as look at and copy files from the Net, send messages to other users, and join in discussion groups.

Once you are online, you can copy new Internet software onto your computer. Find out more about this on pages 32 and 33.

Providing access

Unless the computer you are using is permanently connected to the Net, you will need to find a company that will give you access. This company will act as your gateway to the Net by allowing you to hook up to their computers which are connected to the Net.

Two main types of companies offer this service: Internet service providers and online services.

Internet service providers

A company that provides access to the Net is called an Internet service provider (ISP) or an Internet access provider (IAP). There are many different companies available and more are appearing all the time. You will need to open an account with one. Some may offer you a free trial period of connection to the Net.

Online services

An online service is a company that provides you with access to its own private network in addition to access to the Internet itself. The types of services offered on private networks range from international news to shopping facilities, business information, discussion groups, and a wide selection of entertainments.

Making choices

You'll find the phone numbers of a selection of Internet service providers and online services advertised in Internet magazines and local newspapers, with details of any special offers available. Each company offers different services, software and costs.

Phone up a company to make sure that they will provide the service best suited to your needs. Here are some of the key questions to ask:

Can I access your computer for the cost of a local call?
Large service providers have points of access to the Net all over the country. Each of these is called a node, or a Point of Presence (POP).

Make sure that the service provider you choose has a POP near you, so that you only have to pay for a local telephone call to go online. This will be far cheaper than making a long distance call every time you use the Net.

What will my e-mail* address be?
Each Net user is given a unique address for sending and receiving e-mail. Some people like to use their name or nickname as part of their e-mail address.

Ask a service provider how much choice they can give you in choosing an address.

What costs can I expect?
Make sure that you understand exactly how much you will have to pay for your Internet connection. There is a list of the type of charges you can expect on page 13.

Try to avoid paying start-up costs, as you will lose this money if you decide to change service providers.

Find out whether there is a monthly fee and whether you will be charged for the amount of time you spend online.

If you are using an online service, check what fee you will have to pay for using their special services and their private network.

You can find out about e-mail on page 27.

Costs

Some companies will connect you to the Net for free, others will charge you. Here are some of the costs you will come across:

Start-up cost – You may have to pay to open an account with a service provider.

Monthly fees and **time charges** – In some countries, such as Great Britain, local telephone calls are charged by the second. Most service providers in these countries do not charge for the amount of time a user spends online and only charge a small monthly fee for using their services. Many online services, however, do charge for time spent online.

In countries such as the USA and Australia, where local telephone calls cost a fixed amount or nothing, service providers usually charge for the amount of time a user spends online. This discourages people from staying online all day, preventing others from using the Net.

Software – Some service providers will send you a CD or a number of floppy disks containing all the Internet software you will need to get started. The cost of this is usually included in the start-up fee. Other companies may charge you a fee to copy software from the Net. Find out more about this on page 33.

Opening an account

Once you have decided to open an account, you'll need to give your service provider your name, address and telephone number.

Make sure that you tell them what kind of computer you are using so that they send you the correct Internet software.

What software do you supply?
Different companies supply different Internet software. If a friend has recommended a particular program, you may want to ask if it is available.

Do you provide access for the type and speed of modem I have?
Make sure that the modems (see page 10) used by an service provider can communicate efficiently with your modem.

The speed of the modems they use should not be slower than the speed of the modem connected to your computer.

Do you have enough modems so that I can connect at peak times?
Each person who dials up a service provider's computer needs a separate modem to make their connection. There are certain times of day when a lot of people use the Net. If all a service provider's modems are being used, you will get a busy signal and won't be able to get a Net connection.

Think about when you are most likely to use the Net and ask the service provider what its busiest periods are. Ask what its modem to customer ratio is.

Do you have a help line?
Most service providers have a telephone help line to give you advice on how to install and use your Internet software. Check how much it will cost you to use this facility. Many companies that provide free Internet connections charge a high rate for using their telephone help lines

Connecting and disconnecting

Once you have your equipment set up and your software installed, you are ready to connect up to the Internet for the first time. If your computer is not permanently connected to the Net, you will need to dial up a connection to your service provider's computer.

Dial up a connection

Open the window that contains a menu of the Internet facilities your service provider offers. This window may contain a button or menu item that instructs your modem to begin to dial up a connection. If not, select one of the Internet facilities, such as the World Wide Web, to start up your modem automatically.

This is part of the connection window of a service provider called Pipex Dial.

The Connect button

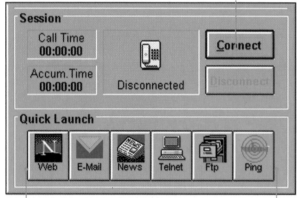

These buttons will start up your modem and take you straight to a particular Net facility.

Password

A box may appear asking you to supply a password. This password will be given to you by your service provider.

Your modem

Once your modem starts working, you may see flashing lights (if the modem is on your desktop) and hear dial tones. When it connects to the service provider's computer, you may hear strange squealing and fizzing sounds.

Connected

Once you are connected, an icon or message will tell you that your dial-up has been successful.

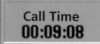

Your window may have a display that begins to time how long you have been connected to the Net.

No connection?

It may be more complicated than you think to get all the software correctly installed and your modem working.

Don't hesitate to ring up your service provider's helpline with any problems. They should be able to help you.

When you are satisfied that your software and equipment are working, you may still be unable to get a connection. A message may appear saying your dial-up has been unsuccessful. Look at page 38 to find out why this may happen.

Warning

With some Internet connections you will automatically be given the choice of disconnecting after a certain period of time. This is a safeguard against spending hours online and possibly running up an enormous phone bill. If your software doesn't do this, be careful not to leave your computer connected to the Net for long periods.

Disconnecting

To disconnect from the Net, select the disconnect button or menu item.

The World Wide Web

The World Wide Web, also known as the Web or WWW, is probably the most exciting part of the Net. Art galleries, magazines, music samples, sports, games, educational material and movie previews are all available on the Web. It's not only interesting, but it's easy to use too.

Web pages and Web sites

The Web is made up of millions of documents called Web pages. These pages are stored on different computers all over the world. A collection of Web pages run by one person or organization is called a Web site. A computer containing one or more Web sites is called a host or server.

Browsers

To take a look at Web pages, you need a piece of software called a browser. If you have the *Microsoft Windows 95* or *Macintosh System 8* operating systems you will probably already have a browser. The software provided by a service provider should include a browser.

Starting your browser

To start your browser, connect up to the Net and select the Web button or menu item in your menu window. Your browser window will open. The *Netscape Navigator* browser window is shown below. Most browsers will have similar features.

When you launch your browser, a Web page may automatically appear in its window. This may be your browser's or service provider's "home page". A home page allows you to see what is available on the other pages that make up a Web site. It is like a contents page, or a store window which shows you what you can buy in the store. It is the page from which you start exploring a site. You will come across many home pages on the Web.

The Netscape Navigator *browser window*

The Home button - Click here to come back to your chosen home page.

The name of the browser

The menu bar contains your menu options.

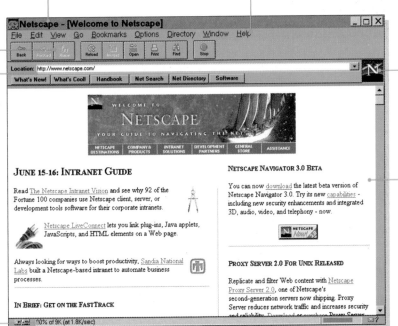

The Location box contains the name of the page currently displayed.

This picture moves while the browser is searching for Web pages.

The window in which the pages are displayed. This is the home page for the company that produces Netscape.

This box displays information about what the browser is doing.

Web pages

The Web is made up of millions of pages of information. Despite its vast size, it's easy to find your way around, because every page has an address and all the pages are interlinked.

Web addresses

The addresses given to pieces of information on the Net, such as Web pages, are called URLs (Uniform Resource Locators). They may look complicated, but they are simple to understand.

The imaginary URL below shows the three main parts of an address:

http://www.usborne.co.uk/public/homepage.htm

The first part, the "protocol name", specifies the type of document the page is. **http://** tells you that the page is a Web page. Some pieces of information have different protocol names, such as **ftp://** (see page 32).

http://www.usborne.co.uk/public/homepage.htm

The second part, the "host name", is the name of the computer on which the page is stored.

http://www.usborne.co.uk/public/homepage.htm

The final part, the "file path", specifies the file in which the page is stored and the name of the directory in which that file can be found.

The URL shown above tells you that the page is a Web page. It is stored on a site belonging to a company called Usborne in the UK. The file containing the page is called homepage.htm, which is found in a directory called public.

⚠ Be careful

When you write down or type a URL, make sure that you copy it exactly. There are no spaces between letters. Take note of where capitals are used and where lower case letters are used.

Finding a Web page

To find a particular Web page for which you have a URL, you need to be online. Type the URL into your browser's window and press the Return key. In *Netscape Navigator* you type the URL into a box named the Location box.

When a page appears in your browser window it is said to have been "downloaded". This means that its contents have been stored in your computer's temporary memory. Even if you disconnect from the Net, you'll still be able to see the page.

Give it a try

Try typing in the following Web address so that you can have a closer look at a Web page:

http://www.nasa.gov/

The home page of the National Aeronautics and Space Administation (NASA) in the USA will appear in your browser's window.

Type the URL in this box.

The Netscape logo moves while the browser is downloading a page.

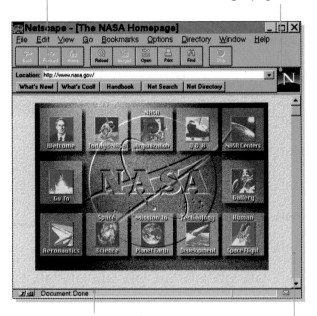

This line shows you the size of an incoming page and how much of it has been downloaded.

Use the scroll bars to view the whole page.

Hypertext

Although pages on the Web may look like the pages in a book, if you look closely they have words and pictures that are underlined or highlighted. These are known as hypertext links. They are used to interconnect all the pages on the Web.

When you point to a hypertext link on a page, your pointer changes into a hand symbol like this.

If you click on the link, a new page containing related information will be downloaded. The link may take you to another page on the same site or to a site somewhere else on the Net.

When you point at a hypertext link, the URL of the page to which you will be transferred is displayed in your browser window.

The picture below shows how you can use hypertext to jump between pages.

This is a hypertext link. Click on this picture to go to a new page.

Clicking on this hypertext picture will take you back to the home page.

Welcome to the Gallery

Pages are interlinked like a vast spider's web.

Photo Gallery

Astronomy

Astronomy Picture of the Day Archive

This link will take you to an ultraviolet photograph of the Earth.

Ultraviolet Earth

Clicking on the underlined words in this list will take you to a selection of photographs.

Floating Free in Space

Browsing the Web

Moving from one page to another on the Web is called browsing, or surfing.

When you have browsed through several pages, you can use the Back and

Forward buttons to go back to previously viewed pages or forward again.

You can click the Home button at any time to return to the home page selected in your browser.

Exploring the Web

There are many interesting sites for you to visit on the Web, but you don't always know where to begin. This section shows you some of the techniques you can use to explore the Web.

Search services

A number of search services on the Web help you to find Web pages with information on specific subjects, without knowing their URLs. There are two main methods they use to search. Some use a key word search system, while others use a series of menus to find the subject you require.

Your browser may have a button or a menu item which brings up a list of the search services available. In *Netscape Navigator*, for example, the button is called *Net Search*.

Net Search

Word search

To use a search service which searches by key word, type in a word or words which describe the subject you are searching for. The search service will then search through its index of millions of pages and present you with a list of pages that contain your word or words.

Say, for example, you wanted to find out about rockhopper penguins using the search service called AltaVista. Go to the AltaVista home page at the following URL:

http://www.altavista.com/

On the home page is a search box. Type in the following: **+rockhopper** and **+penguin** and then click the *Submit* button to start the search.

A list of relevant pages will appear on your screen. Choose one and click on its hypertext link to download the page into your browser.

Use your browser's Back button if you want to return to the list to select another Web page to look at.

AltaVista at work

Click on the hypertext links in the list to jump to new pages.

A list of penguin pages

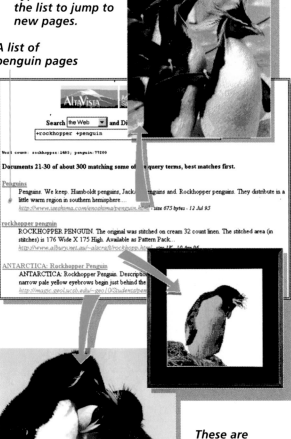

These are some of the pages you will find.

⚠ **Be careful**

Each search service has a slightly different system of entering key words. Make sure you follow the instructions a service gives. This will ensure that you find Web pages which cover the information you want.

Menu search

A menu-based search service divides the information on the Web into subject areas. It gives the user a series of subject menus to choose from, that gradually narrows down the subject area.

Yahooligans! is specially set up to find Web pages that will appeal to young people. It's part of a larger search service called Yahoo!. Go to its home page at:

http://www.yahooligans.com

If, for example, you want to use Yahooligans! to find a museum, click on Art Soup.
From the next menu choose Museums and Galleries. When a list of options appears, click on the hypertext link of the item that particularly interests you.

Using menus to find a Web page

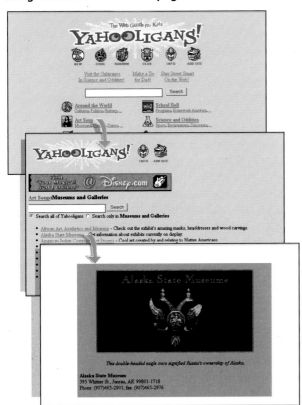

Cool sites

If you don't want to look at anything specific on the Web, you can just sample some of the great things out there in cyberspace. There are several useful places where you will find lists of new and interesting sites.

 Browser buttons Your browser may have a button or menu item that will display a regularly updated list of new and interesting sites. This will contain hypertext links that will take you straight to the Web pages described. In *Netscape Navigator*, for example, there's a *What's Cool* button and a *What's New* button.

 What's New Web pages With the Net expanding rapidly, hundreds of new sites come online every day. There are many Web pages devoted to listing what is new. Some of these are simply a collection of all the new pages, others only include the URLs of pages that the lists' compilers think are worth visiting.

 Magazines and directories You will find a wide selection of Internet magazines and directories available that contain URLs and descriptions of new and exciting Web pages.

Newsgroups and mailing lists If you join online discussion groups called newsgroups (see page 22) and mailing lists (see page 31), you may be guided toward interesting pages by other members of the group. There are newsgroups, such as **comp.internet.net-happenings**, that are specially set up to discuss new sites.

These pages contain tips on how to become a really expert Web surfer. Find out how to find and download pages quickly. You can save text and pictures from Web pages onto your computer's hard disk.

If you have any problems downloading pages, find out some of the causes on page 38.

Speed surfing

Some Web pages take a long time to download, particularly if they include pictures. To speed things up, you can instruct your browser to download only the text on a page.

Your browser should have a menu item called *Auto Load Images*, or something similiar. (In *Netscape Navigator* this is in the *Options* menu.) When this item is selected, images will be downloaded automatically. Make sure this item is not selected. Now, when you download a Web page, small icons will appear in place of any pictures on the page. Be careful. Some pages look a little confusing if you don't download the pictures, and you may find it difficult to use their hypertext links.

This is the picture icon that appears in Netscape Navigator.

Stop!

You can stop a page downloading at any time by pressing the Stop button on your browser.

Bookmarks

As you explore the Web, you'll find pages that you want to look at regularly. Football fans, for example, might want to keep up with their team's latest results. Instead of trying to remember the URLs of these pages, you can add their names to a special list so that you can find them easily.

To add a page to this list, download it. In *Netscape Navigator*, open the menu called *Bookmarks*. Click on *Add Bookmark*. (With other browsers this facility may have a different name, such as Hotlist.) To download a marked page, all you have to do is open the Bookmarks window and double-click on its name in the list.

Netscape's Bookmarks window

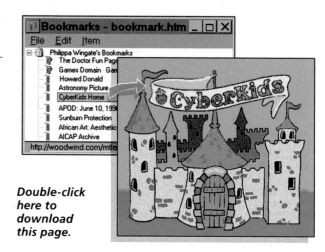

Double-click here to download this page.

Saving Web pages

Some pages disappear from the Web or are changed, so you may want to save certain pages onto your computer's hard disk.

To do this, download the page and select *Save As* in the *File* menu. In the Save As dialog box give your page a filename and specify where you want to save it. In the *Save file as type* section select *Source* and then select *OK*. This saves the page with its layout and hypertext (the pictures are not saved).

To look at your saved page you don't have to be online. Open your browser and select *Open File* in the *File* menu. Select the name of your file and click *OK*.

Save your page using a Save As dialog box.

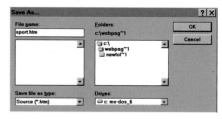

Saving pictures

To save a picture on a Web page, click on it with your mouse (if you are using a PC, use your right mouse button). In the menu that appears, select the option to save the image. In the Save As dialog box that appears, choose a name and location for the picture and click *OK*.

These cartoons have been saved from an Internet football magazine.

Helper applications

As you surf around the Web, you may find files that your browser cannot handle. These pages often include video clips or sound clips. A message box may flash up on your screen telling you that you don't have the right software to view a page correctly. You will need to add "helper applications" to your browser to enable it to handle these files.

The message box usually includes advice about what software you need and how to download it. Follow the instructions provided.

Java™ Programs

Java is a computer programming language that enables Web pages to contain special features. These features include short animations, continually updated information and interactive features. (This means that you can take part in what happens, and choose the things you want to see or hear by clicking on screen.)

You will need to download a Java helper application to see these special features.

A Java program makes the planets on this Web page whizz around.

To find out more about Java, you can visit the Java home page at **http://java.sun.com/**.

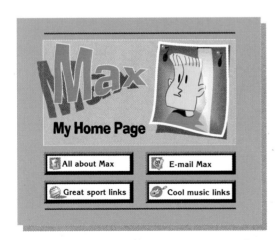

Publishing your own Web pages

Once you become familiar with using the Web, you may find that you want to create your own Web pages. You'll need to find someone who will allow you to store your pages on their computer. Many service providers supply a small amount of space on their computers free with your Internet connection. Alternatively, you can hire space for a small monthly fee.

There are many software packages available which will help you design and construct your own Web pages.

Newsgroups

By joining discussion groups called newsgroups, you can use the Net to get in touch with people who share the same interests as you. Most newsgroups discuss very little actual news – a lot of it is chat and trivia, but it's fun!

Usenet newsgroups

Newsgroups form a part of the Net called Usenet. There are over 25,000 newsgroups available for you to join. Each one has a single theme, covering interests and hobbies, from jazz music to jets, from jokes to jobs.

Some newsgroups are dedicated to discussion, while others are more like helplines where you can ask questions and get advice from the experts around the world.

When you join a newsgroup, a copy of all the articles recently written by members of the group will be sent to you. You can read these articles, write your own, or join in ongoing debates.

Newsgroup names

Each Usenet newsgroup has a unique name. The name acts as a guide to its theme. The name has two main parts. The first part describes what basic topic the group covers, such as science or computing.

The following are the abbreviations used for some of the main newsgroup topics:-

alt.   Alternative newsgroups. These cover all kinds of topics, but usually in a humorous, crazy and alternative way.

biz.   Business newsgroups. These cover discussions of new products, ideas and job opportunities.

comp.   Computing newsgroups. These cover everything to do with computing and computer technology. They are great places to start looking for expert help.

misc.   Miscellaneous newsgroups. These cover subjects such as health, kids, and books which don't fit any other topic group.

news.   Newsgroup newsgroups. These offer tips and advice for people using Usenet for the first time.

rec.   Recreational activities newsgroups. These cover sports, hobbies and games, from skateboarding to sewing.

sci.   Scientific newsgroups. These are mainly used by academics to discuss their research.

soc. and **talk.**   Social and talk newsgroups. These offer the opportunity to discuss and debate social issues, different cultures, politics, religion and philosophy.

The second part of a newsgroup name, known as its subtopics, narrows down the topic area the group concerns. For example, an imaginary newsgroup name might be **rec.music.presley**. This tells you that the newsgroup is in the recreational activities topic group. Its subtopic is music, more specifically the music of Elvis Presley.

Newsgroup access

Most service providers will give you access to Usenet newsgroups as part of your Internet package. They should supply you with a program called a newsreader, which enables you to read and send newsgroup articles.

Some browsers, such as *Netscape Navigator*, include a newsreader facility. For this, you will need to open a special newsreader window.

Opening your newsreader

Once you are on-line, open your newsreader window. First you need to display a list of the names of all the newsgroups available. To do this, select the button or menu item which invites you to view all newsgroups. In the *Netscape News* window, you should select *Show All Newsgroups* in the *Options* menu. A list like the one below will appear.

You need to be online so that you can look at this list. Your computer will download it from a computer called a news server. Once it has been downloaded, you can disconnect while you look at it.

Choosing a newsgroup

Scroll through the list of newsgroup topics, opening topic folders to see which subtopics they contain. If, for example, you wanted to find a group that discussed mountain biking, you would click on **rec.*** to see a list of its subtopics. Next you would click on **rec.bicycles** and, finally, on **rec.bicycles.offroad**.

Subscribing

To subscribe to a newsgroup, simply locate its name in the list and select a subscribe button or menu item. In the *Netscape News* window you click in the box beside the group's name. You don't have to pay to join a Usenet newsgroup.

Unsubscribing

To unsubscribe from a newsgroup, click in the box so that the check mark disappears, or select an unsubscribe button or menu item.

A list of newsgroups in a section of the **Netscape News** *window*

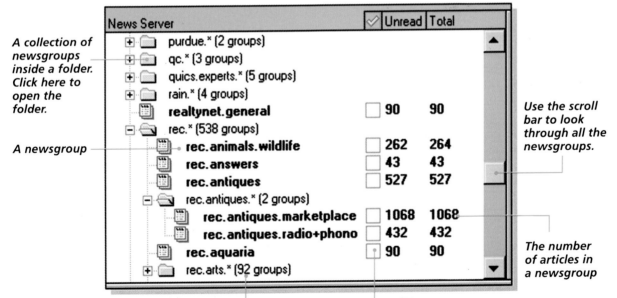

A collection of newsgroups inside a folder. Click here to open the folder.

A newsgroup

Use the scroll bar to look through all the newsgroups.

The number of articles in a newsgroup

This number tells you how many newsgroups this topic group contains.

A mark will appear in this box when you join or subscribe to this group.

Posting to newsgroups

As a new member of a newsgroup, you'll be known as a newbie. It's fun to get involved in debates and discussions or ask for information and advice. On these pages you'll find out how to join in by receiving and sending newsgroup articles.

Collecting articles

Messages sent to newsgroups are called articles or postings. Once you have subscribed to a newsgroup, a computer called a news server will send you a copy of all the articles that have recently been posted to that group.

To collect these articles, you need to be online. Open your newsreader window. A number will appear beside the name of each of the newsgroups you belong to. This number indicates how many new articles are currently available in the newsgroup.

Reading articles

Click on the name of the newsgroup that you want to look at. A list of all the new articles in it will appear. Click on the name of an article to download it.

You should disconnect from the Net before you read articles, because you don't want to pay for a long telephone connection.

Keeping track

Once you have read an article, your newsreader will mark it as "read". This means that the next time you come back to the newsgroup you won't see that message. This ensures that only new articles you haven't read before are displayed in the list.

Check regularly to see if you have received anything from your newsgroup, because most news servers delete articles after a few days.

This is the **Netscape News** *window showing an article open.*

Number of articles currently in each newsgroup

A list of the newsgroups to which the user is subscribed

Click here to see the articles in this newsgroup.

A list of articles in the alt.cybercafes newsgroup

Click to open an article.

This article has already been read.

The text of an article

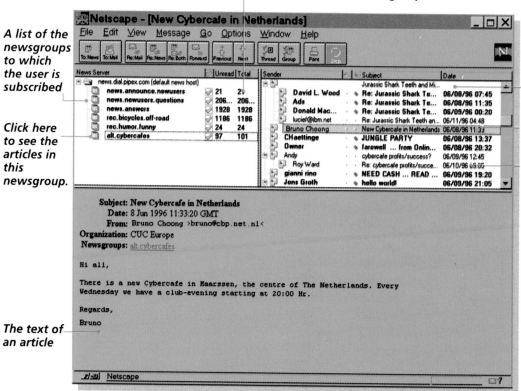

Lurking

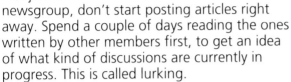

When you first join a newsgroup, don't start posting articles right away. Spend a couple of days reading the ones written by other members first, to get an idea of what kind of discussions are currently in progress. This is called lurking.

Frequently Asked Questions

Most newsgroups have a Frequently Asked Question (FAQ) article. This is a list of the questions most often asked by new members. It saves other members from having to answer the same questions again and again. The FAQ article will appear every couple of weeks. Read it before you start posting.

Ready to post

When you post an article to a newsgroup, you have three options: you can start a new discussion, join in an existing one, or e-mail (see page 27) a personal response to someone else's article. Starting a new discussion is known as starting a new thread. To do this, open your newsreader window. Click on the name of the newsgroup to which you want to send your article. Click the *To: News* button. A message composition window will appear.

Compose your article in a message window.

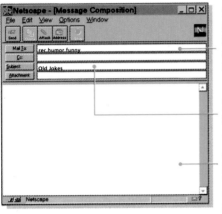

The name of the newsgroup appears here.

The **S**ubject: box

Type your article in this part of the window, called the body.

Summarize the contents of your article in the *Subject:* box, so that people scanning through the list of articles will know if your article will interest them. Write your article in the area of the composition window called the body. For some advice on writing articles, see page 26.

When your article is ready, connect to the Net and select the send button or menu item.

Responding

There are two ways in which you can respond to an existing article. The first is by sending a reply to the newsgroup. This is known as following up. The second is by responding personally to the author of an article by sending them an e-mail. This is called replying.

Open the article you want to respond to. To follow up, select *Re:News*. To reply personally by

e-mail select *Re:Mail*. (It is considered good manners to send an e-mail to the author of an article you are following up. To do this, press *Re:Both*.)

A window will appear in which you can type your message. The *Mail To:* box will automatically be addressed and the body of the message will contain a copy of the article to which you are responding. Edit it down to the points your article is answering.

Compose your message, connect to the Net, and then select the send button or menu item.

> ✉ **Tips**
>
> You can join a newsgroup called **news.announce.newusers** for advice on using Usenet newsgroups.
>
> If you want to check that you are posting articles correctly, you can send a message to **misc.test**. You will automatically get a reply to your message a few days later.

Netiquette

There aren't many rules about what you can and can't do on the Net, but there are things that are considered good and bad manners. Users have developed a code of conduct known as Netiquette. Here are some rules to follow when composing articles for newsgroups or sending e-mail (see opposite).

Keep it brief

Make sure everything you write is brief and to the point. Express yourself as clearly and concisely as you can. People have to download your articles, and the longer they are, the more time and money they will cost to download.

Watch your tone

When you are talking with someone on the telephone, it's easy to know whether they are being funny or sarcastic by the tone of their voice. When typing a message, however, it's hard to show emotion. Some Net users put words in brackets to indicate their state of mind, such as <grin> or <sob>.

Another way of showing emotion on the Net is to use little pictures called smileys or emoticons. They are made up of keyboard characters and when you look at them sideways they are like faces. New smileys are being made up all the time. Here are some useful ones.

:-D	Laughing	:-P	Tongue out
:-(	Sad/angry	:-/	Confused
:-)	Happy/sarcastic	:*	Kissing
:-X	Not saying a word	0:-)	Angel
:-O	Wow!	$-)	Greedy
:*)	Clowning around	:-I	Grim
I-O	Bored	:'-)	Crying

Use an acronym

To avoid too much typing, some Net users have taken to using "acronyms", which are abbreviations of familiar phrases. They usually use the first letter of each word. Here are some of the most commonly used acronyms:

BTW	By The Way
DL	DownLoad
FYI	For Your Information
IMHO	In My Humble Opinion
OTT	Over The Top
POV	Point Of View
TIA	Thanks In Advance
TTFN	Ta Ta For Now
UL	UpLoad
WRT	With Reference To

No shouting and flaming

When you type a message, don't use UPPER CASE letters, because in Net speak this is the equivalent of shouting. It is considered rude and will annoy your fellow Net users. If you break the code of Netiquette or post an article that makes someone angry, you will get "flamed". This means that you will receive lots of angry messages, known as flame mail, from other users.

No spamming

Spamming is Internet slang for sending a huge number of useless or rude messages to a single person or site. The word is also used to describe a technique used by certain businesses which send messages advertising their products to thousands of different users via the Net.

E-mail

Electronic mail, known as e-mail, is a method of using your computer to send messages to other Net users. It's a great way of communicating. With e-mail you can send messages more quickly and cheaply than normal mail. An e-mail sent from London can arrive in Tokyo in under a minute and only cost the same as a local telephone call. Net users call the normal mail "snail mail" because it's so slow!

E-mail addresses

With e-mail, as with normal mail, you need to know someone's address before you can send them a message. Everyone on the Net has a unique e-mail address. When you start an account with a service provider you'll be given your own address.

An e-mail address has two main sections: the username and the domain name. The username is usually the name or nickname of the person using e-mail. (One online service called CompuServe uses a number instead of a name.)

The username is followed by an **@** symbol, which means "at".

The domain name gives information about the computer and its location. (You can read more about domain names on page 8.)

Here's an imaginary e-mail address:

philippa@usborne.co.uk

Username   **Domain name**   **Country**
      At   **Code**

@ Tip

Some e-mail addresses are fairly complicated, so make sure that you write them down *very* carefully.

How does e-mail work?

When you send an e-mail message from your computer, it is delivered to a computer called a mail server. From there, it is transferred across the Net, via a chain of mail servers, until it arrives at its destination.

E-mail software

The software package supplied by your Internet service provider should include a program which will enable you to send and receive e-mail.

Two of the most popular programs currently available are *Eudora* and *Pegasus*. If you are using *Microsoft Windows 95* or *Macintosh System 7*, you will probably already have e-mail software installed on your computer.

An e-mail window

Open your e-mail program window. The example screen shown below is the *Netscape Mail* window. It shows some of the main parts of an e-mail window. Other e-mail program windows will share many of the same features.

The Netscape Mail *window*

These are the folders in which incoming and outgoing mail is stored.

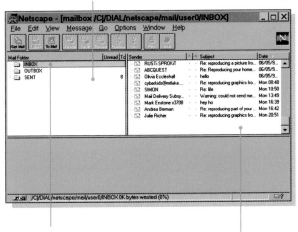

The INBOX folder is open.

This window shows what messages are currently stored in the INBOX folder.

Sending e-mail

On these pages you can discover exactly how to send an e-mail to another Net user anywhere in the world. Find out how to create a handy address book for the e-mail addresses of any friends to whom you want to send messages regularly.

Preparing an e-mail

Open your e-mail program window and select the button or menu item for composing a new message. A window will open. *Netscape Mail*'s Message Composition window is shown below. It consists of a header section and a body section. Type your message into the blank body section. (You will find some advice on writing e-mail on page 26.)

Filling in a header

Before you can send an e-mail you have to fill in the header section. This is like writing the address on the front of an envelope to make sure the letter inside reaches its destination.

In the *Mail To:* box, type the e-mail address of the person to whom you are sending the message. Add the address of anyone you want to send a copy of your e-mail to in the *CC:* box.

Choose an informative subject line to fill in the *Subject:* box. Many Net users receive lots of e-mail, including junk e-mail which is mostly advertising. Use the subject line to give the person who receives your e-mail an idea of what is contained in your message. This ensures that he or she won't just delete the message without reading it. The subject lines appear in a list of messages stored on your computer. They act as a useful reminder of what each e-mail is about.

Netscape Mail's *Message Composition window*

The header section

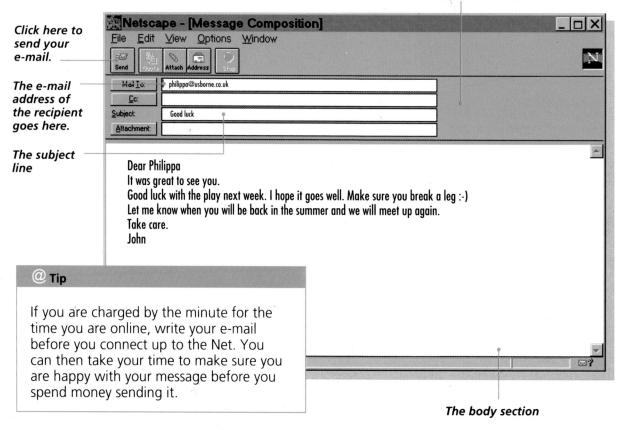

Click here to send your e-mail.

The e-mail address of the recipient goes here.

The subject line

Mail To: philippa@usborne.co.uk
Cc:
Subject: Good luck
Attachment:

Dear Philippa
It was great to see you.
Good luck with the play next week. I hope it goes well. Make sure you break a leg :-)
Let me know when you will be back in the summer and we will meet up again.
Take care.
John

@ Tip

If you are charged by the minute for the time you are online, write your e-mail before you connect up to the Net. You can then take your time to make sure you are happy with your message before you spend money sending it.

The body section

Signing off

Many e-mail programs allow you to create a personal "signature" which automatically appears at the end of your messages.

Your signature can only be made up of letters and symbols from the keyboard. Some people use them to draw complicated pictures, while others will include a funny quotation. You could include the snail mail address and telephone number of your school or company.

The signatures shown below are pretty long. Ideally, you should make your signature no more than four lines. People will have to spend time and money downloading your e-mail file, so a long signature might make you unpopular.

If you want your signature to be included with an e-mail, you have to instruct your computer to attach it.

This signature is a picture made out of keystrokes.

- * - * - * - *

Jessica Hopf
Maxim School
35 Long Street
Townsville
tel 01876 4657

- * - * - * - *

This signature includes a snail mail address.

Sending an e-mail

When you are ready to send an e-mail message, select the send button or menu item.

If you are connected to the Net already, your message should be sent right away. If you aren't connected, your computer will probably save the e-mail. Next time you dial up a Net connection, it will be sent.

Your e-mail program may show an animation to tell you that your message has been sent.

An address book

Many e-mail programs let you create an address book containing the names and e-mail addresses of the people to whom you regularly send messages.

You can type e-mail addresses into your address book, or add addresses from e-mails you have already received.

To send a message to a friend, you usually only have to double-click on their name in your address book. A message composition window that is already addressed to them will open.

Netscape Mail's Address Book window

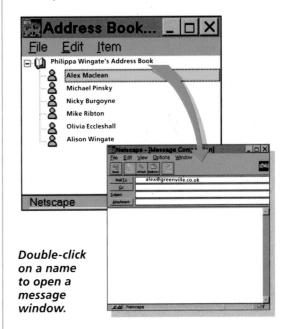

Double-click on a name to open a message window.

Finding an address

There isn't a directory listing the e-mail addresses of all the users on the Net. The easiest way to get someone's address is to ring up and ask them. Get them to send you an e-mail to make sure that you don't write down the wrong address. Their address should appear at the top of their message.

Receiving e-mail

Any e-mail sent to you will be stored in a mailbox by your service provider. You can find out here how to collect, read and reply to it.

Reading an e-mail

To collect e-mail, you need to be online. Open your e-mail window and select the button or menu item that searches for new mail. Most programs have an icon or message that tells you when new mail arrives. Any mail will automatically be downloaded. You can then disconnect from the Net before you read it.

Many e-mail programs place new mail in a folder or in-box. When you open the folder, the messages will appear in a list detailing their sender, subject and date.

To read a message, double-click on its name in the list. It will appear, with a header section specifying its sender, subject and date, followed by the text of the message itself.

Replying to an e-mail

Many programs make it very easy to send a reply. You simply open the message you want to reply to and select a reply button or menu item. In *Netscape Mail*, this button is called *Re:Mail*. A message composition window will appear, with the *Mail To:* box addressed to the sender and the *Subject:* box filled in. The body of the message will contain a copy of the original e-mail. You can delete it or edit it down to remind the sender which message you are replying to.

Bouncing e-mail

Sometimes e-mail doesn't reach its destination. Any e-mail that fails to get through and is sent back to you is said to have "bounced". If your e-mail bounces right away, check that the address is correct. If it bounces after a couple of days, there has probably been an equipment failure on the Net. Try sending it again.

Send yourself e-mail

To try out your e-mail program, you can send an e-mail to yourself. Put your own e-mail address in the *Mail To:* box.

Alternatively, you can e-mail an organization called Mailbase. The address for the USA, Canada & South America is:

mail-server@rtfm.mit.edu

Leave the subject line blank and enter this message in the body:
send usenet/news.answers/internet-services/access-via-email.

Mailbase's address in Europe and Asia is:

MAILBASE@mailbase.ac.uk

Leave the subject line blank and enter this message: send lis-lis e-access-inet.txt

Attachments

Mailbase should send you back an e-mail including an "attachment" which contains more information about e-mails. An attachment is a file added to an e-mail.

It can be a text, a picture or a sound file. To read an attachment you need to select a button or menu item in your e-mail window and follow the instructions you are given.

Mailing lists

A sure way of receiving lots of e-mail is to join one of the many mailing lists available via the Net. They are like newsgroups (see page 22), because you can discuss a wide variety of topics with other enthusiasts, but with mailing lists you send and receive articles by e-mail.

Finding a mailing list

To find an index of the mailing lists available on the Net, open your Web browser and type in the following URL:

http://www.Neosoft.com/internet/paml/bysubj.html

A menu of topic groups, like the one shown below, will appear. When you click on a topic in which you are interested, you will see a list of the mailing lists related to that topic. Click on the name of a list to see a brief description of the types of issues discussed by its subscribers.

A list of mailing lists available on the Net

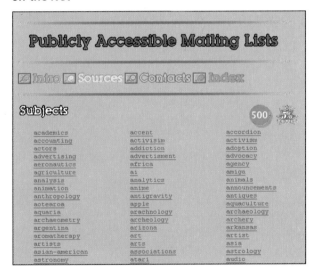

Welcome

After you have subscribed to a mailing list, you should receive a reply to your e-mail within a few minutes or a few hours. Make sure you keep this "welcome" e-mail, as you may need to refer to it. The message will confirm you have joined successfully. It may also give you some rules of the list, the address to which you send e-mail and how to unsubscribe from the list when you want to.

Many mailing lists have administrators who oversee the messages sent in. In your welcome e-mail you may be told the e-mail address of the list administrator. You can e-mail them if you have any specific problems or questions.

What next?

As a member of a mailing list, you will receive a copy of all the e-mail sent to the list. Download these messages in the way you would download any e-mail (see page 30).

Subscribing to a list

The page containing a description of a mailing list should also include instructions about how to subscribe to it. Follow these instructions closely. Each mailing list has a slightly different system. It usually involves sending an e-mail to a specified address, with a specified subject line or message in the body of the e-mail.

Sending e-mail to a list

To send a message to a mailing list, simply compose an e-mail message in the way described on pages 28 and 29. Send it to the address specified in your welcome e-mail.

Make sure you don't send any personal messages intended for the list administrator to the mailing list e-mail address by mistake.

Files via the Net

There are thousands of sites on the Net with files for you to copy onto your computer, from pictures to sound clips, from text files to Internet software. The main method of transferring files over the Net is called File Transfer Protocol (FTP), and the easiest way to use FTP is with a Web browser like Netscape.

Finding FTP files

FTP files are stored on computers all over the world, called FTP sites. They have addresses, called URLs (see page 16) which help you to find them. Their URLs begin with the letters **ftp://**.

When you are browsing the Web, you will probably come across Web pages which have hypertext links to FTP sites where you will find files to download. There's a long list of FTP sites at the following address: **http://hoohoo.ncsa.uiuc.edu/ftp-interface.html**

A good way to find FTP files is using a search service (see page 18) such as Infoseek, Yahoo!, or Lycos.

For example, you could use Infoseek to find a new browser program. Type the words **browser**, **software** and **best** into its word search box and click the Search Now button. In the list of URLs that appear, there might be some suitable FTP files. To download one of these FTP files, you would simply click on the hypertext link.

(Infoseek will charge you for its services, but it offers a free trial period.)

Permission

You often need permission or "authorized access" to download files from the Net, but there are lots of files that are available for anyone to use. These are called anonymous FTP sites, because you don't have to be a known user or use a special password before you copy files onto your own computer.

Using FTP

Whether you type the URL of an FTP site into your browser, or click on a hypertext link to an FTP site, your browser will automatically connect or "log in" to the computer where the files are stored.

Sometimes a file will automatically start downloading onto your computer. Alternatively, you may see a list of all the files available on the FTP site. Find the file you require and then click on it.

Downloading

Before your computer starts downloading a file, a *Save As...* dialog box will appear. You must give the file a name and select where you want to store it. Choose whether you want to save it on the hard disk of your computer or on a floppy disk. Finally, click the *OK* button.

A Save As... dialog box

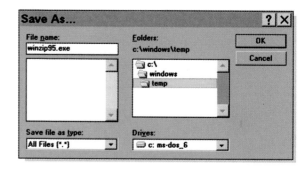

The file will start downloading. A *Saving Location* window will appear giving details about the file you are downloading and telling you how much of it has been downloaded.

A Saving Location box

This shows you how much of the file has already been downloaded.

Zipped up

Many FTP files are compressed or "zipped". This means they have been made smaller, so that they take up less room when stored on a computer's hard disk and can be transferred across the Net more quickly. A file or files compressed in this way is known as an archive.

Once a compressed file is copied onto your computer, you have to "decompress it", restoring it to its original size so that your computer can use it properly. It's a little like a beach ball; you let all the air out of it so that it fits in your bag to take to the beach. But once you are there, you blow the air back into it so you can use it.

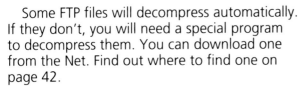

Some FTP files will decompress automatically. If they don't, you will need a special program to decompress them. You can download one from the Net. Find out where to find one on page 42.

Internet software

Much of the latest Internet software is available to be downloaded from the Net. Some of these programs may be better or more up-to-date than the software supplied by your service provider. You may choose to download a new browser, such as *Netscape Navigator*, an e-mail program or a more recent version of a program you are already using.

On page 42 you'll find the addresses of some good software to download.

Is the software really free?

You will have to pay for some of the software you come across on the Net before you can download it. It is usually the same amount of money as if you bought the software package in a store.

There are many programs which you can download by FTP that are either free or available at a very small cost. They fall into three main categories: freeware, shareware and beta programs.

.Freeware This is software that is completely free for anyone to copy onto their computer and use. The person who created the software has donated it free of charge.

Shareware This is software that you can install on your computer, but there are certain conditions attached. The most common condition is that you try out the program for an initial free trial period. If you like it, you then pay the person who owns it. The amount you pay is usually small.

When you have made your payment, the software company usually sends you the manual, notifies you if the software is updated and helps you if you have any problems using it.

Beta programs Beta programs are new programs that have been tested by the company that created them and are available for further testing by users. They may have mistakes and problems in them. If you find a fault (known as a "bug") in the program, you should inform the company who created it. Some beta programs are free; others will be charged for.

Cyberchat

E-mail and newsgroups are great ways of using the Net to make friends and communicate, but you do have to wait for a reply. Sometimes it's only a couple of minutes, but it can be a day or two. Today, there are facilities on the Net that allow you to communicate with other users instantly.

Internet phone

There are programs available that allow you to use your computer like a telephone. The Net can transmit sound in the same way that it transmits any other kind of data.

To talk to a friend on the Net, you will need a microphone, a pair of speakers connected to your computer, and a sound card (see page 11). The person you intend to talk to must have the same equipment. You will both need to download an Internet telephone program and you will have to pay for it.

Once you have installed your equipment and your program, you can dial up your friend's computer. When he or she answers, you can speak, just as on a normal telephone.

This is an Internet phone called WebPhone.

You can dial a telephone number by clicking on these buttons on screen.

One of the great advantages of using an Internet telephone is that you can call anywhere in the world for the price of the local call that connects your computer to your service provider's computer.

Video phones

Internet video phones allow you not only to talk to a person via their computer, but also to see them on your computer screen while you talk.

To use this system you will need a video digitizer and a video camera connected to your computer system. This will film you and transmit the data over the Net to another user. You will also need a microphone, speakers, sound and video cards, and a video phone program.

Conferencing

The Internet telephone and video phone systems described above have been further developed to allow several people to speak and watch each other at once. This enables people to have debates and discussions using the Net.

The quality of the sound and pictures achieved by these programs is getting better as the equipment and the speed of data transfer (see page 11) on the Net improves.

CU-SeeMe is a program used for video-conferencing.

✉ Finding software

You can find out where to go on the Net to download some of the software mentioned in this section in the list on page 42.

Internet Relay Chat

A popular Net facility is Internet Relay Chat (IRC). This allows you to have live conversations with other users, using your keyboard to type your conversations. As you type a message, it instantly appears on another user's screen. He or she can read it and type a reply.

The groups in which people meet to have chats are called channels. Some of them are dedicated to discussions about particular topics, such as football or computer games, while others are used for more general, sociable chat.

The IRC channels are controlled by special computers on the Net called IRC servers, which transmit all the chatting around the world.

IRC programs

To join in IRC, you will need a program called an IRC client program. This will interpret the data supplied by an IRC server. You can download an IRC client from the Net.

IRC is quite complicated to use. There are many codes and commands that you need to type in to tell your computer what you want it to do. So make sure that you read all the instructions that are downloaded with your IRC client program.

Virtual worlds

Another place to meet other Net users is in virtual worlds. These are imaginary 3-D worlds generated by computer. In a virtual world the scenery changes according to how you move. You can use your mouse or arrow keys to walk around. You can interact with things, such as picking up objects or opening doors.

One of the great things about virtual worlds on the Net, is that you will meet other users there. They appear on your screen as "avatars". An avatar is a body that represents a user and moves through a virtual world,

responding to instructions. An avatar may look like a bird, a cat, a goblin, or anything. You can talk to the other users you meet using your keyboard to type in your comments. Your words will appear on the screen for them to read.

An avatar

To enjoy virtual worlds you need special software, a powerful computer (at least a 486DX66 with 16MB of RAM), a fast modem (at least 33,600bps), and a video card.

Avatars in a virtual world called Worlds Chat

Maria

Bruno

Explore a virtual world called AlphaWorld.

Games online

If you like to play games on your computer or games console, there are lots of challenging games on the Net for you to download and play. But the best way of playing games is online.

Finding games

There are lots of places on the Net where you can find out about games. Many big games manufacturers, such as Sega and Nintendo, have their own home pages where you can read about their new products, get some hints and tips about how to play a particular game, and enter competitions.

Alternatively, you can use a search service (see page 18) to find information about a particular game you are interested in.

Here are some of the home pages you will find.

This site has links to video games.

Let's talk games

You can use the Net to get in touch with other games enthusiasts so that you can discuss tactics and expertise. There are many newsgroups and mailing lists dedicated to discussing individual games.

The best place to start looking for games newsgroups is in the **rec.games** folder in the list of newsgroups (see page 22). There are groups for the fans of games ranging from pinball to backgammon.

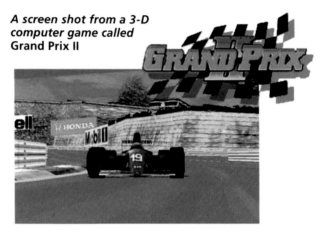

A screen shot from a 3-D computer game called **Grand Prix II**

Off-line games

From chess, to football, there are lots of games on the Net that you can download. Once a game is downloaded and stored in your computer's memory, you don't need to be online to play it.

On the Web page where a particular game is discussed, you will usually find a hypertext link that will take you to a site from which you can download the necessary software.

> ✉ **Useful addresses**
>
> On page 42 you will find a list of the URLs of some of the Web pages shown in this section. You will also find a selection of other great Web sites.

Online games

One of the great advantages of using the Net to play games is that you can play online against other users. For example, a user in Berlin can play online chess against a user in Tokyo. If you prefer fantasy games, you can take part in adventures with other users, fighting against them for prizes or teaming up with them to quest and battle together.

Watch an online chess game or take part yourself.

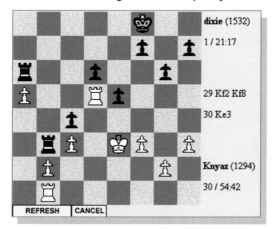

Games software

To play an online game, you need a piece of software called a client. This is a program that enables your computer to communicate with the computer on which a particular game program is running. For example, to play a chess game, you will need a chess client.

You can download games clients from the Net. Sometimes you have to pay to use them. Most games pages have hypertext links to the sites where you can download client software.

Logging on

When you are ready to play an online game, you need to "log on" to the computer where the game program is running. Log on means you gain access to the computer so that you can use the games program stored on it without transferring it to your own computer. A hypertext link on a games page usually enables you to log on automatically.

MUDs

Multi-User Dungeons, known as MUDs, are popular online games. You'll find hundreds of them on the Net. MUD games are adventures that take place in imaginary kingdoms. There are three main types: combat games – where you fight opponents; role play games – in which you play a particular character such as a wizard; and social MUDs - which are based on chatting to other players.

Text or graphics

Most MUDs are text-based. This means that when you meet a monster, you don't see it, you read a description of it. So let your imagination run wild. As you embark on an adventure, text will appear, telling you where you are, what you can see, and giving choices of action. Some MUD games have pictures. They are called graphical or GUI MUDs.

A screen shot from a GUI MUD called Illusia

A screen shot from a GUI MUD called Rubies of Eventide *and (inset) a goblin from* Empires

Problems and solutions

The Internet is sometimes called the Information Superhighway. This description gives many people high expectations of the speed at which information can travel via the Net. Some users are disappointed by problems and congestion which can make the Net slow and frustrating to use. They might call it the Information Dirt-track or the Information Superhypeway.

This section explores some of the problems you may come across on the Net and suggests how to deal with them.

No connection

When you dial up your service provider to go online, you may fail to make a connection. The most common cause of this is that too many people are using your ISP's computer and so there are no lines left available. This often happens at times of the day when a lot of people want to use the Net. Redial a few times, but if this doesn't work, try again an hour later.

If you still can't get a connection, telephone your service provider to check that there isn't a fault with their computer.

If you often find that your service provider doesn't have enough telephone lines to deal with all their customers, you might consider finding a service provider with better facilities.

Losing a connection

Once you are online, a message may appear telling you that you have lost your connection. This is usually due to your service provider's computer failing. Try connecting again.

Problems on the Net

There are a number of reasons why you may be unable to download Web pages or files successfully. Here are some of them.

Equipment failure   The computers and equipment that make up the Net sometimes break down. All you can do is try again later.

Wrong address   A message, such as Host Not Found, may appear on your screen. This usually means that you have typed in the URL incorrectly. Check carefully that you have used the correct upper and lower case letters and punctuation.

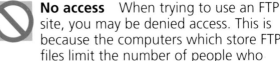

Change of address   You may see a message telling you that the file you require doesn't exist. It may have been removed from the Net, relocated, or had its name changed. Try removing the part of the URL that specifies the exact filename. For example, you might want to look at a photograph with the following address: **http://www.imaginary.co.uk/users/ phil_jones/pix/png32.html**. If you typed this in and the file didn't appear, you should try removing the filename, **png32.html**. This might take you to a list of the photographs available and you could resume your search.

No access   When trying to use an FTP site, you may be denied access. This is because the computers which store FTP files limit the number of people who are allowed to use them at the same time. This ensures that downloading files doesn't get too slow. Try again later.

Software problems   If you can't get your browser to connect to anything, close it down and reopen it. There may be a mistake in the program, called a bug. This is particularly possible if you are using a beta version of a program (see page 33). If the problem persists, report it to the program's manufacturer.

Congestion

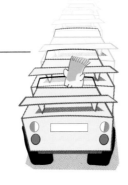

One of the main problems facing the Net is its growing popularity. Every day, more people want to go online and do increasingly complicated things, such as downloading video and sound clips. The result is that the Net gets congested with traffic jams of data. This makes everything move more slowly, just like cars on a busy road.

To cope with this problem, new high-speed connections are being built which can handle more data at greater speeds. But these improvements take time and money.

In the meantime, it's a good idea to avoid the busiest times on the Net, which tend to be when people in the USA are using it. This is because most of the resources on the Net are based in the USA.

🌐 How many?

People have calculated that if the number of Net users continues growing at its current rate, everyone in the world will be online by the year 2001. This is nonsense, of course, because in many countries people can't afford to buy computers.

Cutting costs

Going online doesn't have to be expensive. You don't need to buy a high-speed modem, a super-fast computer or expensive software. Here are some ways in which you can enjoy all the Net has to offer without spending a fortune.

• If your computer isn't powerful, which means that it can't process data quickly, don't use a Web browser, like Netscape Navigator, that can access newsgroups and send e-mail as well as browse the Web. Programs like this are complicated, and will make your computer run slowly. Choose individual programs to use newsgroups, e-mails and FTP. These programs are older and simpler, and will use less of your computer's memory.

• If you don't have a high speed modem, make sure that you minimize the amount of data you need to download.

One way of doing this is to instruct your browser to download only the text of Web pages, not the pictures. You can find out how to do this on page 20.

• Remember that all the programs you will need are available free on the Net.

You can find out the URL addresses of where to go to download some useful programs on page 42.

• If you are charged for the amount of time you are online, always write e-mails and newsgroup articles before you are connected up.

• Avoid using the Net at times of the day when telephone calls are charged at an expensive rate.

• If you only want to use the Net for e-mail or newsgroups, you can use a local company, called a Bulletin Board Service (BBS), or a service provider, to provide you with access to these facilities. This costs less than a full Internet access connection.

Safety Net

With millions of people using the Net, there are bound to be those who misuse it. Here are some useful guidelines that will ensure the Net is a safe place for you to surf.

 Don't give your e-mail address to strangers. You don't want to receive lots of unwanted e-mail. Just think, you wouldn't give your snail mail address to a complete stranger, would you?

 Someone you chat to on the Net may suggest meeting up in real life (known as "boinking"). If you want to go, make sure you arrange to meet in a public place, where you will feel safe.

 You should always be aware that it is easy for people to play pranks or pretend to be something they aren't on the Net. For instance, you might meet an adult pretending to be a child.

 When you send information via the Net, it passes from one computer to another until it reaches its destination. If somebody gained access to a Net computer, they could use your information dishonestly. Don't send personal details, such as your home address, phone number, or financial details, such as a credit card number, via the Net.

There are some Web sites where financial details are safe. The information is coded so that it can't be used by anyone else.

 People are free to publish whatever they like on the Net. So, as well as interesting things, there's also unpleasant, unsuitable and dangerous information out there. Be careful to avoid anything you don't want to look at.

There are programs available that will check the information you download from the Net for offensive words, and block access to certain Web sites.

 Computer viruses are programs which can damage the data stored on your computer. Every day new viruses are being invented by people who want to harm the Net.

Your computer can catch a virus over the Net if you copy files from an infected computer. Make sure that you have anti-virus software installed on your computer. This will check your hard disk for certain viruses. Update this software regularly to catch new viruses.

 Hackers are people who access computer systems without permission. They can link up their own computers to networks, and open private files. By changing the information in these files, they may be able to steal money or goods.

If you have private information stored on your computer, make sure you set up your system to prevent people connecting to it. If you are using a computer at home, it is unlikely that people can access your files.

Net potatoes

Some people predict that by the year 2000, people will spend more time surfing the Net than they spend watching television.

Some Net facilities, such as games and IRC, can become very addictive. Remember, using a computer for any purpose for long periods of time can damage your health.

It's essential to take a ten minute break every hour that you use a computer. This will rest your eyes and other parts of your body.

There's more to life than surfing the Net. So make sure you don't become a Net potato and end up at the receiving end of a common Net insult... GAL, which means Get A Life!

Web sites tour

Search engines

AltaVista
http://www.altavista.com/

HotBot
http://www.hotbot.com/

Lycos
http://www.lycos.com/

OpenText
http://www.opentext.com/

WebCrawler
http://www.webcrawler.com/

Yahoo!
http://www.yahoo.com/

Ask Jeeves
http://www.askjeeves.com/

Search engines for software
http://www.shareware.com/

Encyclopedias and dictionaries

Encyclopedia.com
http://www.encyclopedia.com/

Knowledge Adventure Encyclopedia
http://www. letsfindout.com/

Compton's Encyclopedia Online
http://www.comptons.com/

Microsoft Encarta Online
http://www.encarta.msn.com/

Webster Dictionary
http://www.m-w.com/netdict.htm

Dictionary.com, English words and their foreign equivalents
http://www.dictionary.com/others/

Roget's Thesaurus
http://www.thesaurus.com/

Whatis?, hundreds of definitions of computer words
http://www.whatis.com/

WebNovice, a simple guide to the Internet
http://www.webnovice.com/

Homework help

The following Web sites have been set up especially to provide homework help. Through these sites, you will be able to contact teachers and subject experts with homework questions.

Answers.com
http://www.answers.com/

Homework Help
http://www.startribune.com/homework/

Links to experts
http://www.cln.org/int_expert.html
http://njnie.dl.stevens-tech.edu/ curriculum/aska.html

Schoolwork Ugh!
http://www.schoolwork.org/

Kids Web
http://www.kidvista.com/index.html

Art and literature

Just For Kids who Love Books
http://www.geocities.com/Athens/ olympus/1333/kids.htm

Web Gallery of Art
http://sunserv.kfki.hu/~arthp/ index.html

A. Pintura, Art Detective
http://www.eduweb.com/pintura/

The Children's Literature Web Guide
http://www.acs. ucalgary.ca/~dkbrown/index.html

Science

The Lab
**http://www.abc.net.au/science/
default.htm**

Exploratorium
http://www.exploratorium.edu/

Smithsonian Institution
http://www.si.edu/

National Air and Space Museum
http://www.nasm.edu/

Bradfort Robotic Telescope
http://www.eia.brad.ac.uk/btl/

Sci4Kids
http://www.ars.usda.gov/is/kids/

History and georgraphy

National Geographic Online
http://www.nationalgeographic.com/

HyperHistory
**http://www.hyperhistory.com/online_n2/
History_n2/a.html**

Castles for Kids
**http://www.castlesontheweb.com/search/
Castle_Kids/**

Eyewitness
http://www.ibiscom.com/

CIA World Fact Book
**http://www.odci.gov/cia/publications/
factbook/index.html**

Geo-Globe Interactive Geography
http://library.advanced.org/10157/

Volcano World
http://volcano.und.nodak.edu/

50 States
http://www.50states.com/

Entertainment

Games Domain
http://www.gamesdomain.co.uk/

Nintendo
http://www.nintendo.com/

Sega
http://www.sega.com/

Sky Sports Online
http://www.skysports.co.uk/

Cartoon Network
http://www.cartoon-network.com/

Mr Showbiz
www.mrshowbiz.com/

Internet software

Netscape, with links to browser software
http://www.netscape.com

Microsoft Download Center, with links to
browser software
http://www.microsoft.com/downloads

Programs for compressing and inflating files
PKZip
http://www.pkware.com/
Winzip for Windows
http://www.winzip.com/
Stuffit for Macs
**http://www.aladdinsys.com/
index.html**

WebPhone
**http://www.netspeak.com/products/
webphone.intro.html**

CU-SeeMe
**http://www.cyber-academy.com/
drewlogon/cuseeme.html**

IRC client software
http://www.mirc.co.uk/

A glossary of Internet words

Here's a list of some of the Internet words you may come across and their meanings. The definitions are specific to the use of the words in relation to the Net. Some words have other meanings in different contexts.

Any word that appears in *italic* type is defined elsewhere in the glossary.

acronym Words that are usually made up of the first letters of a phrase or saying, such as BFN, which is an acronym for Bye For Now.

address A description of where to find a piece of information on the Net.

anonymous FTP To transfer files across the Net you need to use *FTP*. Anonymous FTP is when you can transfer them without using a special user code or password.

applet A small program written in a programming language called *Java*. The applet might be inserted into a *Web page*.

application A program that allows you to do something useful with your computer.

Archie A program that helps locate *FTP* files anywhere on the Internet.

archive A file or files that have been grouped together. They may have been compressed so that they are smaller.

article A message sent to a *newsgroup* or a *mailing list*.

attachment A file, such as a picture file, sent with an *e-mail* message.

avatar A small on-screen picture which represents the body of a player in a *Virtual Reality* game.

backbone A link between computers that carries a lot of information very quickly and usually over a long distance.

bandwidth The capacity of a link between computers to transfer data, measured in *bits* per second (*bps*).

beta A newly written program that is made available to be tested by users.

BBS (Bulletin Board System). A system that allows people to leave messages and read messages left by other people.

bit The smallest unit of computer data.

body The part of an *e-mail* in which the message appears.

bps (bits per second). The unit used to measure how fast information is transmitted by a *modem*.

browser A program used to find and look at documents stored on the Net.

chat Conversations held with other users via the Net.

client A program that enables a computer to use the services provided by other computers.

connect time The length of time spent connected to the Net.

country code The part of the name for an Internet computer that indicates what country it is in.

crash A sudden failure in a computer system.

Cybercafés Cafés at which people can use computers to access the Net.

dialer A program that instructs a *modem* to telephone another computer.

dial up Use telephone lines to connect one computer to another to go *online*.

DNS (Domain Name System). A system of giving computers on the Net names that are easy for users to remember.

domain Part of the name for an Internet computer that specifies its location and whether it is in a commercial, educational or government organization.

down The word used to describe computer equipment that is not working.

download To copy files from another computer onto your own computer.

e-mail (electronic mail). A way of sending messages via computers.

emoticon *see* **smiley**

encryption Using a secret code so that people cannot read files without permission.

FAQ (Frequently Asked Questions). A document used by *newsgroups* which lists the answers to the questions commonly asked by new members.

follow up An *article* sent to a *newsgroup* commenting on a previously posted article.

freeware   *Software* that is free to use.
FTP   (File Transfer Protocol). The system used to transfer files from one computer to another over the Net.

Gopher   A program which searches the Net for information by picking options from menus.
GUI   (Graphical User Interface). A system that uses on-screen pictures which can be clicked on with a mouse to give a computer instructions.

hacker   Someone who gains unauthorized access to a computer to look at, change or destroy data.
hardware   The equipment that makes up a computer *network*.
header   The information at the start of a document that tells a computer what to do with it. An *e-mail* header, for example, contains information about the address of the recipient and the sender.
helper application   A program which enables a *browser* to perform extra tasks, such as playing sound clips.
hit   When someone looks at a *Web site*. The number of hits a particular page receives is counted to see how popular it is.
home page   An introductory page containing links to other pages on a *Web site*. The page that a *browser* displays when you start using it, is also called the home page.
host   A computer connected to the Net.
HTML   (HyperText Mark-up Language). The language used to create documents on the *World Wide Web*.
HTTP   (HyperText Transfer Protocol). The system used to transfer *hypertext* documents over the Net.
hypertext   A document that contains high-lighted text or pictures linked to other documents. When you click on hypertext, the linked document will be *downloaded*.

icon   A picture you can click on to make your computer do something, or which appears to indicate that your computer is doing something.
Internet (or the Net)   A computer *network* made up of millions of linked computers.

Internet service providers (ISPs) also known as **Internet access providers** (IAPs)   Companies that sell Net connections to people.
IP   (Internet Protocol). The system used to specify how data is transferred over the Net.
IP address   The unique number given to each computer on the Net.
IRC   (Internet Relay Chat). A way of having a conversation with other Net users by typing messages and reading their responses.
ISDN   (Integrated Services Digital Network). A type of high speed telephone line which can transmit data between computers very quickly.

java   A language used to write programs which enables *Web pages* to include interesting features such as animations.

link   1. A connection between two computers. 2. The highlighted text or pictures in a *hypertext* document.
log   A file which keeps a record of the files you have used and changed, things that have happened and messages received during an *online* session.
log on/log in   Connect a computer to another computer.

mailbox   The place where *e-mail* is kept for a user by an *Internet service provider*.
mailing list   A discussion group where articles are posted to members of the group via *e-mail*.
mail server   A computer that handles *e-mail*.
menu   A list of options from which a user selects.
MIME   (Multipurpose Internet Mail Extensions). A way of sending files attached to *e-mail*.
modem   (MOdulate/DEModulate). A device that allows computer data to be sent down a telephone line.
moderated   A *newsgroup* or *mailing list* in which articles sent in are not immediately sent out to all the users. First they go to a person, who decides whether they are suitable.
MUD   (Multi-User Dungeon). A game which lots of people can play at the same time, if they are all connected, via the Net, to a computer that is running the game.

network   A number of computers and other devices that are linked together so that they can share information and equipment.

network computer   A special computer designed exclusively to be used on a *network* such as the Net.

newsgroup   A place where people with the same interests can *post* messages and see other people's responses.

newsreader   A program that lets you send and read the messages in *newsgroups*.

node   Any computer attached to the Net.

offline   Not connected to the Net.

online   Connected to the Net.

online service   A company that gives you access to its private *network*, containing various kinds of information, and usually gives you access to the Net.

packet   A chunk of information sent over the Net.

page   A document or chunk of information available on the *Web*.

plug-in   A program you can add to your *browser* that enables it to perform extra functions, such as displaying video clips or 3-D images.

POP   (Point Of Presence). A point of access to the Net, usually a computer owned by an *Internet service provider*.

post   Placing a message in a *newsgroup* so that other members can read it.

protocol   A set of rules that two computers agree to use when communicating with each other.

serial port   The part of a computer through which data can be transmitted. *Modems* are connected to computers through serial ports.

server   A computer or the *software* on a computer, that makes itself available for other computers to use.

set-top box   A special piece of computer equipment that connects to your TV and lets you access the Net using the TV as a screen.

shareware   *Software* which you can try out before you have to pay for it.

signature file   A file, often a picture or a quotation, attached to the end of an *e-mail*.

site   1. A collection of *Web pages* set up by an organization or individual. 2. A computer *network* that is joined to the Net.

smiley   A picture, made up from characters on the keyboard, which looks like a face and is used to add emotion to a typed message.

software   Programs that enable computers to carry out certain tasks.

subscribe   Add your address to a *mailing list* or *newsgroup*.

TCP/IP   The language which computers on the Net use to communicate with each other.

Telnet   A program that allows you to connect your computer to another computer so that you can interact with it. This might mean using its database, or playing a multiplayer game (see *MUD*).

thread   A sequence of articles sent to a *newsgroup* forming a discussion on a particular subject.

timeout   When a computer gives up attempting to carry out a particular function, because it has taken too long.

up   A word used to describe a computer that is functioning.

upload   To copy programs from your computer onto another computer on the Net.

URL   (Uniform or Universal Resource Locator). The system by which all the different resources on the Net are given an address.

Usenet   A collection of *newsgroups*.

Virtual Reality   (VR) The use of 3-D computer pictures (called graphics) to create an imaginary world which surrounds a user.

virus   A program specially designed to interfere with other programs and files.

World Wide Web (also known as **WWW** or the **Web**)   Part of the Net made up of pages of information linked together by *hypertext* links.

zip   A program used to compress files to make them smaller.

Net slang

Lots of slang words are used in connection with the Internet. Here are some of the most common ones.

All the words that appear in *italic* type are defined in the glossary on pages 43 to 45.

boinking   Meeting face to face someone with whom you have made contact on the Net.
bounce   When *e-mail* fails to get through to its destination.
box   A computer.
braindump   Saying everything you know about a topic, but more than your audience really wants to hear.

clickstream   The path you take around the Net by clicking on *hypertext* links.
Cyberspace   The imaginary space that you travel around in when you use the Net.

dead tree edition   The paper version of a book or article that is also available on the *Net*.

electronic anarchy   The state of freedom and lawlessness that exists on the Net. There are few rules and restrictions, so you can do and say what you want.
electrotransvestism   Pretending to be a member of the opposite sex when sending messages over the Net.
eyeball search   To read a page on-screen.
eye candy   Programs which look nice, but aren't particularly useful.

flame bait   A controversial *newsgroup* message that is likely to attract angry messages.
flame mail   Angry or rude messages sent to a member or members of a *newsgroup*.
flame war   An argument carried out by members of a *newsgroup*.

gronk out   What you do when you have had enough of using the Net and stop for the day.

Infobahn, Information Superhighway
Slang words for the Internet.

lurking   Reading the messages sent to a *newsgroup* without sending any yourself.

Net cop, **Net judge** or **Net police**   Someone who thinks it is their duty to tell other Net users how to behave. These terms are usually insults.
Net evangelist   Someone who tries to persuade other people to start using the Net.
Net guru   An expert who is respected for their knowledge of the Net and how it works.
Netiquette   Rules about the proper way to behave when using the Net.
Net surfer   Someone who travels around the Net looking for interesting places to visit and people to talk to.
Net surfing or surfing on the Net   Exploring the Net by jumping from one file to another, like a surfer catching one wave and then another.
Net traffic   Data moving around on the Net.
Net users - Netters, Netsters, Netizens Netheads, Netoisie, Internauts, Infonauts   Names for people who use the Net.
newbie   A new Net user or a new member of a *newsgroup*.
newbie hunting   Looking out for new Net users who aren't sure of what they are doing, and teasing them.
noise   An ongoing conversation in a *newsgroup* Noise usually implies that it is a conversation which isn't very relevant to the topic of the *newsgroup*.

shouting   Writing messages in UPPER CASE letters lets everyone know that you are angry.
snail mail   Normal mail delivered by the post office, as opposed to *e-mail* sent over the Net.
spamming   Sending lots of messages to a *newsgroup*, a *mailing list* or an individual.

virtual journey   The imaginary distances you travel to sites on the Net, even though you stay in one place.
virtual relationship   A friendship or relationship that starts on the Net.

wired   Feeling odd from having spent too much time staring at a computer screen. It can also simply mean connected to the Net.

Acknowledgments

Screen shots

Every effort has been made to trace the copyright holders of the material in this book. If any rights have been omitted, the publishers offer their sincere apologies and will rectify this in any subsequent editions following notification.

Usborne Publishing Ltd. has taken every care to ensure that the instructions contained in this book are accurate and suitable for their intended purpose. However, they are not responsible for the content of, and do not sponsor, any Web site not owned by them, including those listed below, nor are they responsible for any exposure to offensive or inaccurate material which may appear on the Web.

Microsoft, Microsoft Windows, Microsoft Internet Explorer and Microsoft FrontPage are registered trademarks of Microsoft Corporation in the US and other countries. Screen shots and icons reprinted with permission from Microsoft Corporation.
Netscape, Netscape Navigator, and the Netscape N logo are registered trademarks of Netscape Communications Corporation in the US and other countries. Netscape Messenger and Netscape Composer are also trademarks of Netscape Communications Corporation, which may be registered in other countries.
Cover   With thanks to NASA; GP500 Motorcycle Racing game. © 1999 Hasbro Interactive, Inc. © 1995-1999 Dorna; CU-SeeMe is a registered trademark of White Pine Software, **www.wpine.com**;
Activeworlds.com, Inc.; Europe Online; US National Libarary of Medicine.
p.6/7   Rusti Sprokit. All rights copyright © 1996 crisp wreck. Unauthorized reproduction and/or sale is prohibited and subject to intergalactic criminal prosecution. Used by permission.
WebPhone is a trademark of NetSpeak Corporation.
http://www.netspeak.com/
RadioNet. Copyright © 1996 T.P.I. GmbH - the mediaw@re company - designed by Klaus Eisermann
http://www.radio-net.com/hpengl.htm
Visible Human Project
http://www.hlm.nih.gov/
The White House for Kids
http://www1.whitehouse.gov/WH/kids/html/ kidshome.html
The Art of China
http://pasture.ecn.purdue.edu/~agenhtml/agenmc/
CU-SeeMe is a registered trademark of White Pine Software,
http://www.wpine.com/
AlphaWorld. Copyright © 1995-1996 Worlds Inc.
http://worlds.net/alphaworld/
The original unofficial Elvis home page
http://sunsite.unc.edu/elvis/elvishom.html
Cyberkids. Copyright © 1995-96 Mountain Lake Software, Inc. Used with permission.
http://www.cyberkids.com/
Eurostar. Used with permission.
http://www.eurostar.com/eurostar/
World Bank. Copyright © The International Bank for Reconstruction and Development/The World Bank
http://www.worldbank.org/
Europe Online weather map. Copyright © 1996 Europe Online S.A
p.9   Computer Network connections on the NSFNET © NCSA, University of Illinois/Science Photo Library
Cyberia Paris. Copyright © Frederick Froument

p.12   CompuServe   **http://www.compuserve.com/**
Demon   **http://www.demon.net/**
Pipex   **http://www.uunet.pipex.com/**
Individual Network e.V.   **http://www.north.de/ings/**
America Online   **http://www.aol.com/**
p.14   Pipex Dial screen shots © Pipex Dial is a registered trade mark of the Public Exchange Ltd trading as UUNET Pipex. All rights reserved.
P.16/17   With thanks to Nasa **http://www.nasa.gov/**
p.18   AltaVista. Copyright © 1996 Digital Equipment Corporation. All rights reserved.
http://altavista.digital.com/
p.19   YAHOOLIGANS! and the YAHOOLIGANS! logo are trademarks of YAHOO!, Inc. Text and artwork copyright © 1996 by YAHOO!, Inc. All rights reserved.
http://www.yahooligans.com/
With thanks to Alaska State Museums
http://ccl.alaska.edu/local/museum/home.html
p.20   Cyberkids. Copyright © 1995-96 Mountain Lake Software, Inc. Used with permission.
http://www.cyberkids.com/
p.21   Copyright © When Saturday Comes, 1996
http://www.dircon.co.uk/wsc/
Cosmix Solar System, Philip Hallstrom / philiph@cosmix.com. Copyright 1996, Cosmix Web Design
http://www.cosmix.com/playground/java/planets/
p.34   WebPhone is a trademark of NetSpeak Corporation. Patents pending.
http://www.netspeak.com/
CU-SeeMe is a registered trademark of White Pine Software,
http://www.wpine.com/
p.35   Alpha World and Worlds Chat screenshots. Copyright © 1995-1996 Worlds Inc.
http://www.worlds.net/overview
p.36   Nintendo. Copyright © Nintendo of America, 1996
http://www.nintendo.com/
Sega. Copyright © 1995 SEGA, P.O. Box 8097 Redwood City, CA 94065. All Rights Reserved.
http://www.segaoa.com/
Sailor Moon Support Site. Copyright © 1996 Sailor Moon Support Site.
http://www.hkstar.com/~chimo/
Grand Prix II. Copyright © Microprose Ltd.
http://wwwlmicrosrose.com/gamesdesign/gp2/
p.37   Caissa Online Chess. Copyright © 1995-1996 Mediawest Online. Caissa's Web is a trademark of Mediawest Online.
http://caisa.com/info.html
Illusia. Copyright © 1995 Living Mask Productions
http://www.illusia.com/illusia.html
Empires. Copyright © 1996 Dan Bradley
http://ucsu.colorado.edu/~woehr/
Rubies of Eventide. Copyright © 1996 by Cyber Warrior, Inc. All rights reserved.
http://www.cyberwar.com/rubies.html

Computer equipment

Cover   Hewlett-Packard Pavilion Multimedia PC courtesy of Hewlett-Packard; p.10/11   Online Media set-top box produced by Acorn Computer Group plc; Gateway 2000 computer used by permission of Gateway; ACCURA™ 288 Message Modem and the OPTIMA™ V.34 + FAX PC Card were supplied by Hayes Microcomputer Products, Inc., the inventor of the PC modem.

101 THINGS TO DO ON
THE INTERNET

In this section of the book you'll find 101 projects which will help you to discover the fantastic variety of things you can do on the Internet.

When you are connected to the Internet you will have a huge range of information and resources available to you. Each project will show you something fun to do, or teach you a new skill to make using the Internet easier.

TACKLING THE PROJECTS

The projects in this section of the book are divided into themes such as space, films and food, so that you can easily find information that interests you. You can tackle the projects in any order, dipping into the book wherever you like. Each project will give you all the information you need to complete it, or you will be directed to a page where you can find extra help.

HOW DO I GET ONLINE?

To carry out the projects in this book, you will need a multimedia computer, a modem, and a telephone line (see pages 10 and 11).

You will also need to be connected to the Internet. To do this, you'll need a company called an Internet service provider described on pages 12 and 13. Some well-known service providers are *AOL*, *MSN* and *Prodigy*. You could ask friends who use the Internet which ISP they use. If you buy an Internet magazine such as *Wired*, *.net* or *Byte*, you will find advertisements for ISPs, detailing their services and giving telephone numbers to contact.

Some useful questions to ask an ISP are listed on pages 12 and 13. Once you have selected a company, it will send you instructions about how to set up your equipment. It will provide you with the software you need to get connected to the Internet, and instructions about installing it on your computer.

If you have problems with your computer hardware or software, your ISP will have a helpline which you can call for advice.

USING THIS SECTION OF THE BOOK

Once you have an Internet connection, most of the projects in this book can be done using programs that you probably already have on your computer.

The instructions in this section are aimed at personal computer users with *Microsoft®* *Windows®95*. But it doesn't matter if you haven't got exactly the same programs as the ones described here. Most programs of the same type work in a similar way, although the commands may be slightly different. Projects that require an additional program include instructions about how to get hold of the relevant software.

Most of the images in this section were obtained from the World Wide Web. They look a bit blurry, like the images on a computer screen.

In the first section of this book you found about the Net. On these pages there is a brief reminder of the different facilities available on the Net. The main areas the projects in this section of the book cover are the World Wide Web, e-mail, online chat, newsgroups and mailing lists.

When you are connected to the Net, you gain access to this information. You can use it to find out about people and places, to buy things, to communicate with a variety of other people, and to make new friends.

CYBERSPACE

When you use the Net, you travel through an imaginary space called cyberspace. When you visit different places and talk to people, you are moving in cyberspace.

THE WORLD WIDE WEB

The World Wide Web, also known as the Web or WWW, is made up of millions of documents called Web pages. These pages can include text, still and moving pictures, and sound.

Most organizations on the Web have sets of pages which are linked together. These sets of pages are called Web sites.

The Web is the fastest-growing part of the Internet, with hundreds of new pages appearing each day. You can use it to get up-to-date information about almost any subject.

Every Web page has its own address, called a URL (Uniform Resource Locator). This makes it easy to find pages and go back to pages you've visited before.

This is an imaginary URL:

http://www.usborne.com/home.html

This tells you that the page is a Web page.

This tells you the name of the computer on which the page is kept.

This tells the computer the filename of the page.

This URL tells your computer that the page is called *home.html*, and that it is stored on a computer at *www.usborne.com*.

The Web has pages about almost any subject.

You can visit museums and be a tourist on the Web.

You can go shopping on the Web.

Lots of Web sites help people to do research work.

There are thousands of games on the Web.

Governments use the Web to give people access to information.

E-MAIL

Electronic mail, or e-mail, is a method of using your computer to send messages to other Net users. You can contact people, no matter where they are in the world, in a few minutes. It only costs the price of a local telephone call to send and receive messages.

ONLINE CHAT

Lots of people use the Net to chat online. You can type a message onto your screen which is then seen by other users. You can use your computer to talk on the telephone and even take part in a videoconference, where you talk to a person and see them at the same time.

The Net is creating a huge variety of new ways to communicate with other people.

NEWSGROUPS AND MAILING LISTS

There are two kinds of discussion groups available on the Internet: newsgroups and mailing lists.

Newsgroups are Net discussion groups. They work like bulletin boards – users leave messages in a newsgroup which other people can read and respond to.

Many people discuss their interests using Net mailing lists. Mailing list members exchange ideas via e-mails.

Newsgroups and mailing lists deal with all sorts of interests, from science fiction to gymnastics. You can use them to find out more about an interest you have, find other people who share your interest, and leave messages for a whole group of people. There are over 25,000 newsgroups, and a similar number of mailing lists, on the Net.

To use the Internet, you must have a computer, a modem, and a telephone line. You normally have to find an Internet service provider (see page 51) to get connected to the Net.

WHAT TYPE OF COMPUTER?

You don't have to have a high-powered computer to use the Net. You can connect to the Net as long as your PC has at least a 486 processor chip. If you have a Macintosh, it should have a 8036 chip, or better.

Computer memory and storage space is measured in megabytes (MB). Your computer needs at least 16MB of RAM (Random Access Memory) to use Internet and Web software.

Software, and information you want to keep permanently, is stored on your computer's hard disk. Your computer needs at least 200MB of free hard disk space to store Internet and Web software.

This diagram shows how a computer connects to the Internet.

WHAT IS A MODEM?

A modem is a device which enables computers to communicate with each other via telephone lines. A computer produces data in the form of pulses of electricity known as digital signals. A modem converts digital signals into waves that can travel along telephone lines. These waves are known as analog signals.

There are two types of modems that can be used with desktop computers: internal modems and external modems. An internal modem fits inside your computer. An external modem is connected to your computer by a cable which plugs into a socket at the back of your computer. This socket is called a serial port.

Modems transfer data to and from the Internet at different speeds. The speed is measured in bits per second (bps). It is a good idea to use a modem which works at a speed of at least 33,600 bps. The faster your modem works, the less time you will spend transferring information from the Net onto your computer.

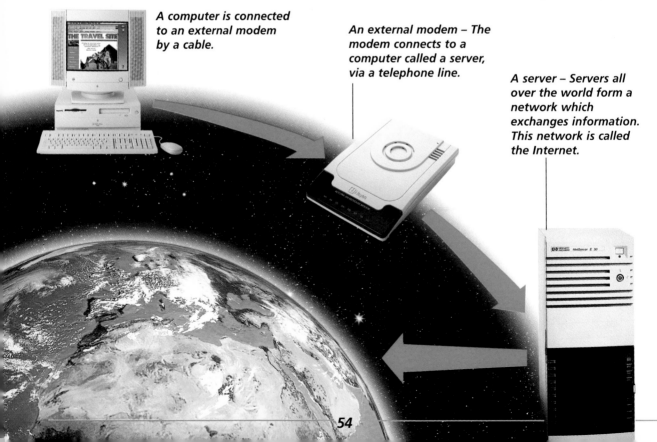

A computer is connected to an external modem by a cable.

An external modem – The modem connects to a computer called a server, via a telephone line.

A server – Servers all over the world form a network which exchanges information. This network is called the Internet.

EXTRA EQUIPMENT

For some of the projects in this book you'll need extra equipment.

These extra pieces of hardware all connect to your computer via cables.

Printer

Web camera

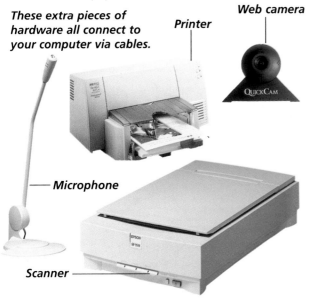

Microphone

Scanner

To print Web pages, pictures or text, you'll need a printer. Alternatively you could take a floppy disk containing documents to a printing and copying business that can print them for you.

If you have a multimedia computer, it will probably be equipped with speakers and a sound card, so that you will be able to hear music or sounds via the Net. If you don't want to disturb other people around you, you could use headphones instead of speakers.

To record sounds and save them on your computer you'll need to have a microphone. You can connect this to your computer.

To convert pictures into files, so that you can view them on your computer or send them via the Net, you will need a machine called a scanner. There's more information about scanners in project 89.

A Web camera is a type of video camera which can be linked to your computer. It records pictures which are broadcast directly onto your computer, and can be sent via the Net. Lots of Web sites show live pictures from Web cameras.

Some games require a graphics card to show 3-D effects.

INTERNET SOFTWARE

When you arrange your Internet connection with a service provider, they will send you instructions on how to get the software you'll need. Most companies send the software on CD-ROM.

Internet software is regularly updated. You can update the software on your computer by downloading the latest versions of programs free of charge from the Web. You may also find software updates on the CDs that come with many Internet-related magazines.

BEFORE YOU START

As you do the projects in this book, you will create new files on your computer. It's a good idea to create a folder on your computer's hard disk or C drive, where you can keep all the documents you make using this book. This way you won't lose track of anything you've produced using the Net.

To create your own folder, click on *Start* and select *Programs*. Select *Windows Explorer*. You'll see a window showing the folders stored on your computer.

Go to the *File* menu and select *New*, then *Folder*. In the right-hand window you'll see a new folder with the title *New Folder* highlighted. Name your folder *Projects* by clicking on the title and typing in the name.

A browser is the program which you use to look at Web pages. You will probably have one included with your Internet software. The two most frequently used browsers are *Microsoft® Internet Explorer*, shown here, and *Netscape Navigator®*. They both work in a similar way.

The **Microsoft Internet Explorer** **browser window**

Use the **Back** **button to see the last page you looked at.**

Pages are displayed in this area.

Web page title   **Use the Stop button if you decide you no longer want to download a particular page.**   **Menu bar**   **Address box**

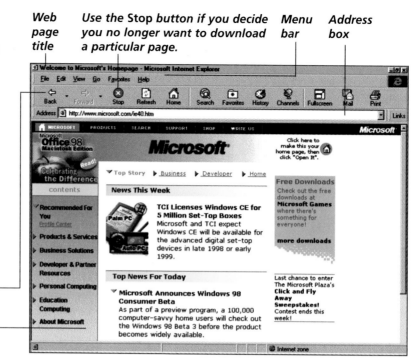

1 GO TO A WEB PAGE

The easiest way to find a Web page is to type its address into your browser's address or location box. Connect up to the Net and start up your browser. Click in the address box and delete the URL if there is one showing. Type in the URL for the White House's Web site: **http://www.whitehouse.gov/**, and press *Enter*. Your browser will download the entry page of the White House's Web site. A site's entry page is called its home page.

This is the White House's home page.

2 SHORT CUT TO A WEB PAGE

When you find a Web page you like, you can create a short cut in your browser so you can find it again quickly. These short cuts are called "Bookmarks" in *Netscape Navigator*, and "Favorites" in *Microsoft Internet Explorer*. They are useful, because URLs are not easy to remember. It's a good idea to create a short cut whenever you find a page that you like. This makes it easier to remember sites and visit them again later.

To create a short cut in *Netscape Navigator*, download your chosen page, go to *Bookmarks* on your menu bar, and select *Add Bookmark*. To look at the Web page which you've bookmarked, simply click on its name from the *Bookmarks* menu while you are connected to the Internet.

To create a short cut in *Microsoft Internet Explorer*, download the page and select *Add to Favorites* from the *Favorites* menu. To view the Web page later, click on its name from the *Favorites* menu while you are online.

There are so many pages and sites on the Web that it's easy to be swamped with information.

The best way to find pages with specific information is by using a program called a search service. There are two types of search service. One looks for Web pages that contain particular words. This type of search service is called a search engine or index. The other kind, called a directory, breaks down Web sites into categories and lists sites in each one. This type is useful for more general searching.

Search services are compiled by teams of editors, or by computers which sift through, and categorize, Web sites. Because there is so much material being added to the Web all the time, no search engine can list every Web site. When you are looking for information on a particular subject, it's a good idea to use at least two services to ensure you get a selection of relevant pages. Some services tell you about new, interesting, or popular sites. Many services also have their own news and weather pages.

SEARCH SERVICE WEB SITES

Search engines
http://www.altavista.com/

http://www.
webcrawler.com/

Directories
http://www.hotbot.com/

http://www.mckinley.com/

http://www.infoseek.com/

http://www.excite.com/

http://www.yahoo.com/
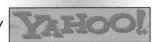

http://www.lycos.com/

(3) CARRY OUT A KEY WORD SEARCH

One way to search is by using key words. A key word is a word which sums up the subject of a page, or which appears a number of times on it.

Open your browser, connect to the Internet, and type in the URL for Webcrawler, at **http://www.webcrawler.com/**. Webcrawler is a search engine. You will see a box where you can type in your key word. This is called a query box. Try typing the word **chimpanzee** into the query box. Click on the *Search* button.

The search engine will compile a list of Web pages which contain that key word. The results are presented as a list of links. At the top of the list you'll see the number of results. Click on a link to visit one of the Web pages.

A search using Webcrawler

Type your key word here.

Click on Search.

A page of results

Click on a link to see a page.

A linked page about chimpanzees

4 SEARCH BY CATEGORY

When you search the Web using a directory, you gradually narrow down the subject area of the page you're looking for. You can do this using Yahoo! at **http://www.yahoo.com/**.

Say, for example, you want to see a page about a television cartoon. Start by clicking on *News & Media* on Yahoo!'s home page. A page of *News & Media* sub-categories will download. Select *Television*, and from the page which downloads, select *Shows*. On the next page, click on *Cartoons*. You will see a long list of titles of cartoons. Select one to view a list of Web pages devoted to that cartoon. Finally, choose a link and click on it to see the page.

Using the Yahoo! directory to find cartoon sites

5 PERSONALIZE A SEARCH ENGINE

Some search engines allow you to create a personalized page. This page will contain news about subjects that interest you, and you can add other information such as forthcoming birthdays and links to interesting sites.

You can create a personal page using Webcrawler (**http://www.webcrawler.com/**). From the home page, follow the link to *My Page*. You will see a sample of a personal page. Select *Personalize* and a form will download. Fill in this form, or click on *Form for non-US residents* if you live outside the USA. You will need to type in your town and region, your e-mail address, and a password. Click on *Submit Registration* when you've finished.

A second form will appear where you can specify the news and information you want to see on your personal page. You can select sections such as *Headline News*, *Entertainment News*, *Weather*, and *Movies*. Make your selections and click on *Submit Interests*.

Your personal page will appear. Click on the *Change* button next to any of the sections if you want to change the information which is shown on the page.

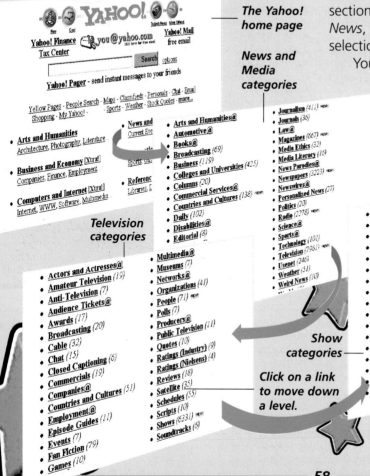

The Yahoo! home page

News and Media categories

Television categories

Show categories

Click on a link to move down a level.

As you move through the directory levels, the subject areas become more specialized.

6 DO AN ADVANCED SEARCH

Sometimes when you search using only one key word, it will produce thousands of results. If this happens, you can narrow down your search by doing an "advanced search". The best search engine for very detailed searches is AltaVista, at **http://www. altavista.com/**.

A common method of performing an advanced search is to look for a specific name or phrase on a Web page. To do this you put quotation marks around the words. For example, to look for a Web page about a person called Maria Dixon you would type in **"Maria Dixon"**.

If you want to find a Web page featuring several words which don't necessarily appear together, put a **+** sign in front of each word. For example, you could find a page about the vaccinations you need if you are going to Indonesia by typing in **+vaccinations +Indonesia**.

You can use similar methods to exclude pages. So if you want to search for a Web page about travel vaccinations, but you don't want information about rabies, use the **-** sign, as in **+vaccinations -rabies**.

An advanced search using AltaVista

Type the search words in the box and click on the Search button.

A results page

1. **Bali Health & Safety**
   Planning Ahead   Health & Safety   Transportation   Traveler's Directory   Special Travel Needs ...
   ✉ *http://www.expedia.msn.com/wg/places/Indonesia/Bali/TEHSBD.htm* - size 4K - 14-Oct-97 - English - *Translate*

2. **20th Century Martyrs**
   20th Century Martyrs. Brutal Worldwide Christian Persecution. by Fran D. Lowe. From the primitive jungles of Communist China and Vietnam to the isolated...
   ✉ *http://www.fnu.com/heritage/may97/Martyrs.html* - size 9K - 21-Dec-97 - English - *Translate*

3. **UK Air Traffic Engineers Travel Society - UKATETS**
   Some of the links from this page are PASSWORD PROTECTED to allow only registered members access. To obtain your USER ID and PASSWORD contact...
   ✉ *http://www.zetnet.co.uk/ukatets/memaery.htm* - size 2K - 2-Oct-96 - English -

Click on a link to see a Web page.

CHANGING WEB ADDRESSES

Because the Web is developing so quickly, it is common for URLs to change. You may find that URLs listed in this book have changed by the time you use them. If you find that a Web site has moved, use a search service to find it, or a similar site if it has been removed altogether. Search using the name of the site, or a suitable key word.

A list of cartoons

- Real Ghostbusters
- ReBoot@
- Ren and Stimpy *(8)*
- Road Rover *(4)*
- Robotech *(53)*
- Rocko's Modern Life *(12)*
- Rocky and Bullwinkle *(5)*
- Roland Rat - about Roland Rat and his friends Errol the Ham Glenis the Guinea Pig and Little Reggie.
- Rugrats, The *(12)*
- Sam and Max - official site about the Fox cartoon.
- Samurai Pizza Cats
- Scooby Doo *(27)*
- She-Ra *(5)*
- Shirt Tales, The
- Simpsons, The *(443)* NEW!
- Sky Dancers - Queen Skyla and her academy students fight to from the threat of Vortex and its master Sky Clone.
- Smurfs, The *(19)*
- South Park *(124)* NEW!

The official Rugrats home page on the Nickelodeon site at http://www.nick.com/ and http://www.nickelodeon.co.uk/

E-mail is a great way to keep in touch with people and is one of the most popular features of the Internet. The projects here will help you use e-mail and find new people to exchange messages with.

Your service provider (see page 55) will probably have given you an e-mail program. The projects in this section use *Netscape Messenger*, which is provided with *Netscape Communicator*, but you will find that other e-mail programs work in a similar way.

7 FIND AN E-PAL

Everyone who is connected to the Internet has an e-mail address. This identifies where their messages will be sent to. Here is an imaginary e-mail address:

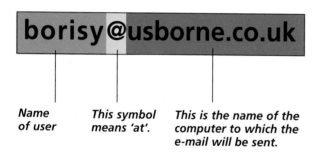

borisy@usborne.co.uk

Name of user

This symbol means 'at'.

This is the name of the computer to which the e-mail will be sent.

If you don't know anyone who has an e-mail address, but you want to send someone a message, you need an e-pal. An e-pal is like a pen friend, but instead of writing letters to each other, you exchange e-mails.

One place to find an e-pal is at the Kids' Space Connection Web site at **http://www. KS-connection.com/**. From the home page, click on *Penpal Box*. You will see a list of letter-boxes for e-pals of different ages. Click on one of these to download a page containing a list of e-pals and their e-mail addresses. Each person on the list has written a short message about their interests. To send an e-mail to one of them, note down their address and follow the instructions in project 8. Make sure you read the site's guidelines about messages.

8 SEND AN E-MAIL

E-mail is very quick and cheap to use, because it only costs the same as a local phone call to send messages. It usually takes only a few minutes for a message to reach its destination.

To send some mail, open your e-mail program. A window similar to the one shown below will appear.

The **Netscape Messenger** *window*

Click here to create a new e-mail.

Button bar

When you receive mail, the titles of messages will appear here.

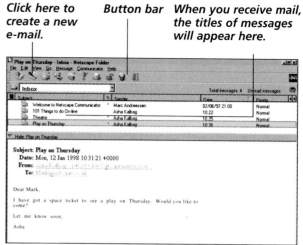

Click on the *New Message* button to create a new message. A window like the one below will appear. Click in the address box and type in the e-mail address of the person you're sending it to. Click in the main box and type your message. Think of a title for the e-mail and type it in the *Subject:* box. Go online and click on the *Send* button to send the message.

Netscape Messenger's Composition *window*

Click here to send the e-mail while you are online.

Type the address in here.

Give the message a title.

Type your message in here.

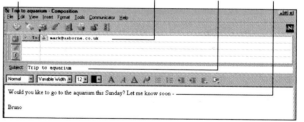

9 DESIGN AN E-MAIL SIGNATURE

Some e-mail programs let you make your messages more personal by adding a special signature to them. This could be a picture made from letters and numbers, or it could include a quotation or joke.

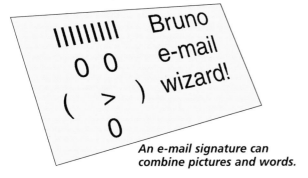

An e-mail signature can combine pictures and words.

You can use any word processing program to design a signature. Start a new document and type in the text you would like to use. Try to make it no more than four lines long, so that it doesn't take too long to download. Select *File*, then *Save*, and give the file a name.

Next, you need to instruct your e-mail program to attach the signature to all your messages. Open up your e-mail program. If you are using *Netscape Messenger*, select *Edit* then *Preferences*. The *Preferences* dialog box will open. Double-click on *Mail & Groups* and click on *Identity*. Select *Choose* to find your signature file, highlight it, and click *OK*. Your signature will be added to each e-mail you send.

10 SEND AN ANIMATED MESSAGE

You can send an animated e-mail message to someone using the Activegram site at **http://www.activegram.com/**. From the home page, click on *Sentiments*. You will see a list of categories including *Birthdays* and *Greetings*. Click on one of these to see a set of pictures. Select one to see it moving.

When you find an animated picture you like, scroll down the page and fill in the online form to send it to someone.

This animated message shows a dog eating a piece of toast.

If you know what type of computer and e-mail program you're sending the message to, fill in these details on the form. If not, click beside *Not Sure*. When the form is complete, click on *Email It Now!*. When the person receives the e-mail, the animated picture may appear automatically. If not, the e-mail will contain the URL of a Web page on which they can find the animation.

SAFETY

Be careful what information you give out in e-mails and in your e-mail signature. Don't include a signature containing your address or telephone number on e-mails you send to strangers. *Never* arrange to meet anyone you get to know over the Internet.

The Internet gives you access to a huge variety of programs that you can copy, or download, onto your computer. These two pages show you how.

Some programs can be added to your browser to enable it to show particular features of Web pages, such as video clips or interactive games. This type of program is known as a plug-in. If a Web page has been created using a plug-in which you don't have, you'll usually see a link to instructions on how to get it when you download the page.

11 DOWNLOAD A PLUG-IN

RealPlayer™ is a plug-in which enables you to listen to sound clips and watch video images via the Net. For example, you can use it to listen to most Web radio stations and hear sound clips on many music sites. You can download it from **http://www.real.com/ products/player/**.

From the home page, click on *RealPlayer*. You will see a form that asks for your name and information about your computer system. This will ensure that you download the most suitable version of the program for your computer. When you have completed the form, click on *Download FREE RealPlayer*.

Next you will see a page with links to sites around the world. Select the link to the site geographically nearest to where you are.

You will see a *File Download* window. Select *Save this program to disk* and click on *OK*. A *Save As* window will appear. Browse through the folders on your C drive and select the *Temp* folder as the save destination. This file should appear with the main ones on your C drive, like *System* and *Programs*.

SECURITY WARNINGS

Some Web pages require you to enter words onto them. For example, you often have to type in information before you download a program, or when you use search services. When you try to send information across the Internet in this way, your browser may display a window warning you that the information is not secure. This means it could be seen by somebody else. If you follow the safety guidelines throughout this book, it will be safe for you just to click *OK* in this window.

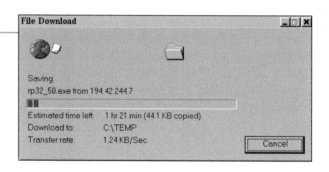

The **File Download** *window*

A new *File Download* window will appear. This tells you the name of the program file and gives you an estimate of how much time it will take to download. A *Download complete* window will appear when the program has been downloaded successfully. Use project 12 to install *RealPlayer* on your computer.

GETTING STUCK

There are lots of different ways of installing programs so the instructions on these pages may not work for every program that you download. You will usually find full installation instructions for a particular program on the Web site that features it, or in a *Help* or *Read Me* file that downloads at the same time as the program files.

12 INSTALL A PLUG-IN

A program such as *RealPlayer* (see project 11) will normally automatically install itself on your computer if you carry out the following instructions. Make sure you are off-line and your browser is closed. Open *Windows Explorer* (to find it, click on *Start* and then *Programs*), and find the *Temp* folder where you saved *RealPlayer's* program file. Double-click on this to start up the installation process.

You will see a *Setup* screen. This gives you the instructions you'll need to install *RealPlayer*. Click on *Next* after you read each screen, and fill in any information, such as your name and e-mail address, when you are asked for it.

An *Installation* screen will appear. This will tell you where the *RealPlayer* program will be installed on your C drive. This is usually a folder called **C:\Program Files\Real\Player** or **C:\Real\Player**. Click *Next* to continue.

You will see a list of the browsers on your computer. (You'll probably only have one.) Place a mark in the box next to each browser listed and click *Next*. On the next screen, click *Next* and then *<Finish>*.

A *Progress* window will appear while *RealPlayer* is being installed on your computer. You'll see a window telling you when the installation process is complete.

13 UNZIP A PROGRAM

Most programs you download will be in the form of "zip" files. These are files that have been compressed so that they take up less room when stored on a computer's hard disk. They can also be sent across the Net more quickly. Zip files have filenames ending in *.zip*.

One place where you will come across zip files is the GamesDomain site at **http://www.gamesdomain.com/**. This has lots of games which you can download. When you find a game you would like to try out, use the method described in project 11 to download its file.

Before you can use a program that has been zipped, you need to decompress or unzip it. To do this, you will need a program called *WinZip* if you use a PC, or *Stuffit* if you use a Mac. You can download *WinZip* from **http://www.winzip.com/** and *Stuffit* from **http://www.aladdinsys.com/**.

The following instructions explain how to unzip a zip file with *WinZip 6.3*. Open *WinZip*. You'll see a license agreement. To continue using the program, click *I Agree*. The *WinZip Wizard* window shown here may appear on screen. (If it does not, select *Wizard...* from the *File* menu in the window that does appear.)

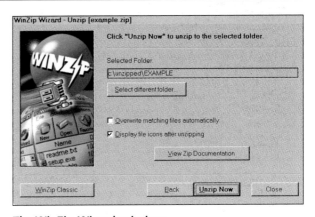

The WinZip Wizard *window*

Winzip Wizard will guide you through the process of unzipping the program and installing it on your computer. During this process, you'll see a list of zip files stored on your computer. You'll need to select the name of the zipped game file you downloaded. *Winzip Wizard* will tell you where it will store the program on your computer when it has finished. It usually unzips programs into a folder called **C:\Unzipped**.

When you want to play the game, use *Windows Explorer* to find this folder and look for a filename ending in *.exe*. Double-click on this filename to start the game.

Your travels on the Internet
need not be confined to the
planet Earth. From the safety of your
computer, you can explore deep space,
visit Mars, look at far-flung galaxies, and
ask astronauts all about their lives.

(14) VISIT THE SURFACE OF MARS

There are thousands of fascinating
pictures of the planets in our galaxy on the
Web. NASA's Web site contains a large range
of pictures from space. NASA is the USA's
space agency. It runs all of America's space
missions, and controls the information which
comes back from them.

To see pictures of Mars, start up your
browser and connect to the Net. Type in the
URL for NASA: **http://www.nasa.gov/**. Your
computer will download NASA's home page.

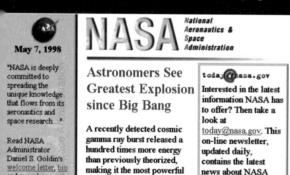

NASA's home page

Scroll down the page, and click on the link
to *Multimedia Gallery*. From the menu which
appears, select *Photo Gallery*. You will see a list
of different subject areas. Click on one of these
to see a page with a set of small pictures. Click
on one to see a larger version of the image.

You can find pictures of the surface of
Mars by clicking on *Space Science* on the NASA
home page, then *Missions*, and *Mars
Pathfinder*. You will see a page with
information and pictures.

To make sure you see the most recent
photographs available, you can use a search
engine to find material which has only just
been added to the Web. AltaVista's Advance
Search feature at **http://www.altavista.co**
allows you to search the Web by date. Type
a key word (see project 3), in this case **Mars**
in the main box. To find Web sites about M
updated within the last month, type in the
date one month ago in the *From:* box. Type
today's date in the *To:* box. Click on *Search*
for a list of Web sites.

These pictures of Mars first appeared on Nasa's Web site in 1997.

(15) LOOK AT PICTURES FROM SPACE

The Hubble space telescope has been transmitting pictures from Earth's orbit since 1993. You can look at some of these pictures on the NASA Web site (**http://www.nasa.gov/**). Click on the *Multimedia Gallery* link, and then the *Photo Gallery* link. Scroll down to *Astronomy*, and use the *Space Telescope Science Institute/Hubble Space Telescope Public Release Images* link to see a menu of pictures.

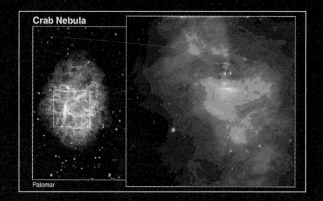

Hubble pictures from NASA's Web site

The picture menu is made up of a set of small pictures known as thumbnails. When you click on one, the computer downloads a larger version of the image. Web sites with lots of graphics, like NASA's, often use thumbnails to save people from spending a long time downloading images they don't want to see.

You can find out more about Hubble on NASA's Starchild site at **http://starchild.gsfc.nasa.gov/**.

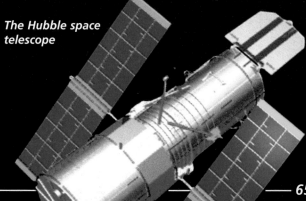

The Hubble space telescope

(16) CONTACT AN ASTRONAUT

Have you ever wondered exactly what it is like to live in space? Now you can ask astronauts about their food, or how they sleep when they're weightless, by sending questions to them using an online form.

The Ask An Astronaut home page at http://www.nss.org/askastro

There are several Web sites which let you contact astronauts. The National Space Society Ask An Astronaut Web site at **http://www.nss.org/askastro/** contains interviews with different astronauts on a regular basis. You can submit your questions, and after a few weeks the astronaut will answer some of the questions which people have asked. The answers appear on the Web site.

On the Ask An Astronaut home page, click on the hyperlink to *Submit Your Question!*. A form will appear for you to fill in your name and e-mail address. Many Web sites use online forms like this. Information is sent via the Internet like an e-mail, but using the Web instead of a separate e-mail program. When you have filled in the form, click on *Submit Question*.

Don't forget to check back on the Web page to see whether an astronaut has answered your question.

There's a wealth of information about the natural world on the Net. You can get advice on looking after your pet, and contact organizations who provide information about different types of animals and plants, and how to protect them.

(17) GET HELP WITH YOUR PET

Whatever pet you have, there's bound to be helpful information about its breed, and how best to care for it, on the Web. A good place to search for this is Acmepet, at **http://www.acmepet.com/**. This Web site, like many others, has a built-in search facility, which

works like a search engine. From the home page, search the site by typing the breed of your pet into the *Search* box and clicking on *Search*. You'll see a list of links to relevant articles.

Pictures of animals in their natural habitats taken from the Web

(18) SEND A PICTURE WITH AN E-MAIL

You can use the Internet to send and receive pictures. One of the easiest ways to do this is by attaching them to e-mail messages.

One place to find amazing photographs is the American Museum of Natural History's endangered species Web site. This site contains information about rare animals, such as cheetahs and rhinoceroses. It's at **http://www.amnh. org/Exhibition/ Expedition/Endangered**. It is important to type this URL with the capital letters shown here.

Ann's Photo Gallery at http://www. inmind.com/people/amartin/ has pictures of wolves like this one.

When you have found a picture to send, click on it with your right mouse button. Select *Save Image As* (or something similar) from the menu which appears. In the next dialog box, select the *Projects* folder you created on page 55. The picture will already have a filename, so you can simply click on *OK* to save it. To attach the picture to an e-mail, open your e-mail program. Create a new e-mail (see project 8), and compose your message. Click on *Attachment*. Select *Attach File* from the new window. In the next window, browse to find the name of your saved picture file. Select it, and click on *OK*. When you are ready, connect up to the Net, and send the message in the usual way.

19   PRINT A PICTURE FROM THE WEB

You can print out pictures you find on the Web to use in projects. Say, for example, you wanted to print out a picture of a parrot. To find a picture, you could try the Online Book of Parrots at **http://www.ub.tu-clausthal.de/ 2p_welcome.html**.

Save your chosen picture using the method described in project 18. In the *Save as type* drop-down list, select *Bitmap*, add *.bmp* to the filename, and click on *Save*. Now disconnect from the Net. You don't need to be online while you print out your picture.

Before you can print out your picture, you need to open it in a graphics program such as *Paint*. To do this, start up *Paint* then select *Paste From* on the *Edit* menu. A window will appear. Browse to find the picture file, and click on *OK*. Your picture will appear on screen. Select *Print* from the *File* menu to print it out.

You may want to make changes to a picture before you print it out. For example, you could add some words to turn it into a poster. You can use *Paint* to do this.

You can print any of the pictures you find on the Web. This picture shows two macaws with bright plumage.

20   SIGN AN ONLINE PETITION

Many Web sites allow you to get involved with campaigns and make your voice heard by signing online petitions. One of the largest wildlife organizations is the World Wide Fund For Nature (**http://www.panda.org/**). It has Web sites in a lot of countries and often uses online petitions to press for changes.

A selection of the conservation sites available on the Web

National Wildlife Foundation at http://www. nwf.org/

Treasured Earth Network at http://www. ten.org/

WWF-UK at http://www.wwf-uk.org/

The online petitions produced by organizations such as conservation groups normally consist of a statement or request with an online form attached. To add your name to the petition, fill in details, such as your name and e-mail address, on the form. Then click on a *Send* link. The organization creating the petition will deliver it to the government or person at which it is aimed. The more names that are on it, the more likely it is to be noticed.

The Web is a rich source of information for fans of all kinds of sports. You can use the Net to find out latest scores, get news about a team, or find out about future sporting events.

21 PREVIEW A FUTURE EVENT

The Web is a useful resource for finding out about events that haven't happened yet. For example, the next Olympics will be held in Sydney, Australia, in the year 2000, but you can already visit its Web site at **http://www. sydney.olympic.org/**.

To get some information about the sports at the 2000 Olympics, click on the logo to go to the home page, and click on *Sports*. You will see a list of the sports which will be included in the Games. Click on one of these, for example *Gymnastics*, to see a page with more information about that sport.

The logo for the Sydney 2000 Olympics

22 FIND SPORTS STARS

Many famous sportsmen and women have more than one Web site devoted to them. They are likely to have an official site, set up with their permission and cooperation and a number of "unofficial" Web sites, usually created by their fans.

You could try finding an official site about the tennis player Pete Sampras using a search engine. Type in his name, plus the word **official** as your key words (see project 3). To find a selection of unofficial sites, simply omit the word "official".

The official site about Olympique Lyonnais, a French soccer team

23 GET THE LATEST SCORE

News agencies and broadcasting companies often maintain Web pages which are constantly updated with sporting information and results. One very thorough online sports service is CNN/Sports Illustrated at **http://www.cnnsi.com/**.

Explore the site to find information about a sport that interests you. To ensure that the information on a page you are looking at is completely up-to-date, you should click on your browser's *Reload* button from time to time. This will instruct your browser to download the latest version of the Web page, which should contain the current scores or results.

24 FIND A SPORTS MAILING LIST

You can exchange messages about sports with other enthusiasts by joining a mailing list. This is a discussion group which sends e-mails to people interested in a particular subject. Some mailing lists deal with individual teams, others cover whole sports.

To help you find the name and e-mail address of a mailing list about a particular subject, there is a search engine called Liszt at **http://www.liszt.com/**. The Liszt Web site includes links to Web pages with instructions on how to subscribe to, and use, particular mailing lists.

Find mailing lists using the Liszt home page.

25 JOIN A SPORTS MAILING LIST

Joining a mailing list is as easy as sending an e-mail. Some lists have their own Web sites which tell you exactly what to do. You normally have to send an e-mail with the word *subscribe* in the title to a particular address. You can find the e-mail address for a mailing list using Liszt, as in project 24.

When you join a mailing list, you will normally be sent an e-mail with all the essential information about the list. This will include how to send your own e-mails to everyone on the list, and how to unsubscribe from the list.

The London-based soccer club Chelsea has a Web site at http://www. chelseafc.co.uk/.

Like most soccer teams, Chelsea soccer club has a mailing list. Its e-mail address is chelsea@cogs.susx.ac.uk

MAILING LIST TIPS

• You should expect to wait a day or two for a response to any messages you send to a mailing list.

• Create a separate folder in your e-mail program to hold your mailing list e-mails.

• Follow the mailing list's guidelines about the kind of messages you can send in.

• Unsubscribe if you are going on holiday, and resubscribe when you get home, or you may end up with hundreds of e-mails.

It's possible to listen to radio broadcasts and recordings over the Net, as well as making your own music online. You can also join a newsgroup (see page 53) to debate with other Net users who share your interests.

26 JOIN A MUSIC NEWSGROUP

To join a newsgroup that discusses the kind of music you enjoy, you will need a program called a newsreader. Most browsers include a newsreader. The instructions in this book are for *Netscape Collabra*, which is part of *Netscape Communicator*. (In this program newsgroups are called discussion groups.)

The first time you use newsgroups, you need to download a list of the ones available. To do this, start up your newsreader and go online. From the main screen, click on the *Subscribe* button. The *Subscribe to Discussion Groups* window will appear, and it will download a list of newsgroups. This can take several minutes.

Netscape Collabra's Subscribe to Discussion Groups *window*

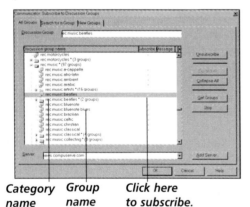

Category   Group   Click here
name   name   to subscribe.

When the list has downloaded, you'll see a list of categories, for example **rec** and **sci**. Each one contains several newsgroups. The name of a category describes the type of newsgroups it contains. For example, **sci** contains newsgroups in which science is discussed. Categories are shown as folders and newsgroups are represented by a speech bubble icon.

Click on the **+** sign next to a category folder to see a list of the newsgroups it contains. Most newsgroups about music are in the **alt** (alternative) and **rec** (recreational activities) categories. When you see the title of a newsgroup you'd like to join, such as the one shown below, click in the *Subscribe* column next to its title. Click *OK* to return to the main news screen

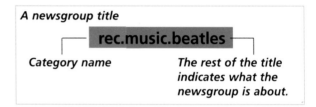

A newsgroup title

rec.music.beatles

Category name   **The rest of the title indicates what the newsgroup is about.**

To read the messages in a newsgroup, you need to know the name of your news server. This is the computer that gives you access to newsgroups. You can find out what it is called by asking your service provider (see page 51). On the main news screen, click on the **+** symbol next to the name of your news server to see a list of all the newsgroups to which you have subscribed. Double-click on the name of one of them to download the titles of its messages, known as postings. Highlight a title to read a posting.

The Netscape Collabra *window*

Tool   Menu of   **Titles of postings**   **The text of**
bar   newsgroups   **to rec.music.**   **a posting**
                      beatles   **appears here.**

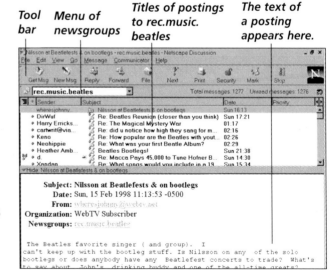

NEWSGROUP TIPS

• Look out for a message called Frequently Asked Questions or FAQ. This is a list of the questions most often asked by new members. Read this before you start sending messages to a newsgroup.
• If people send messages you don't like, leave the newsgroup.
• Never give out personal information such as your surname, address, or telephone number.

27 DISCUSS MUSIC VIA THE NET

You can give your opinion on a song by sending a message to the newsgroup you found in project 26. Sending a message to a newsgroup is called posting. Before you do this, read the other postings to the newsgroup over a few days. This is called lurking. It's a good idea to lurk so you don't post an inappropriate message.

To post a message, click on *To News* on your newsreader's toolbar. A window will appear in which you can type your message.

28 LISTEN TO WEB RADIO

Many radio stations have Web sites where you can listen to broadcasts online. You will need to download a plug-in to hear them. This is usually *RealPlayer*. (See project 11 for information on downloading this plug-in.)

Once you have downloaded *RealPlayer*, go to a Web radio site. You will find Britain's Virgin Radio at **http://www.virginradio.co.uk/**. Follow the *click here* link on its home page. On the page which appears, click on *RealPlayer 3.0*. The *RealPlayer* window will open, and you will hear the station through headphones or speakers attached to your computer.

29 MAKE MUSIC ON THE WEB

You can create your own music, and work with other musicians, using a program called *DRGN* (the Distributed Real-time Groove Network). You can download this from the Net for free.

To download *DRGN*, visit the Res Rocket site at **http://www.resrocket.com/**. Select *Getting Started* to get basic information about using the program. Click on *Software & Support*, then *Download DRGN* to start downloading it. On the next screen, select *download via WWW*. Use the instructions in projects 11 and 12 to download and install it. Click on the *Next* button on the page while it's downloading. Fill in the form which appears to select a password to use with the program.

DRGN comes with complete instructions. Read these carefully. You can use *DRGN* to create music tracks using the keys on a computer keyboard. You select the instrument you want to sound like, and select the notes you want to play. You can then join other musicians in an area called a *DRGN* studio. Together, you can combine different tracks to create a song. Musicians call this a "jamming" session.

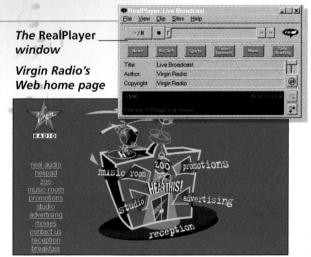

*The **RealPlayer** window*

Virgin Radio's Web home page

There are lots of ways to use the Internet to help you do research, write essays, or get assistance with your homework. You may want to find some extra facts or a good picture to add to your work. If you do find a Web site useful, don't forget to mention its name and address in your work to show that you've used it.

Sites designed to help with your homework

30 ASK EXPERTS FOR HELP

There are many sites on the Web where you can get help from experts on a range of subjects, from science to art.

The Homework Help site at **http://www.startribune.com/homework/**, for example, invites you to send in questions and get a personal reply from a teacher.

Imagine, for example, you needed to find the answer to the question "Which insect species has the longest life cycle?" On the home page, click on the *Science* link. First you should check that the question hasn't already been asked. To do this, click on *search engine*. A search page will appear. Type in the word **insects** and click on *Search*. You will see a page showing a list of people who've asked questions about insects. Click on a name to read that person's question and the answer.

Once you are sure that nobody else has already asked your question, return to the main *Science* page and click on the *Zoology* link.

On the next page, click on *Animals*. You will see a list of relevant questions and answers.

To ask your question, scroll down to the online form at the bottom of the page. Click on the name box and type in your first name. Next, click on the question box and type in your question. Press *Post My Message* to send your question to the site. The question will be posted onto the Web page. The Homework Help site tries to answer questions within 24 hours. Check back later to see if an answer has been posted.

Don't forget that when you contact teachers for help they need time to respond. If they're in another country, there may be a time difference of several hours. So don't expect a reply immediately.

A page showing questions and answers

31 LISTEN TO OTHER LANGUAGES

You can learn some foreign words or phrases by listening to them being spoken on Web pages. One site where you can do this is the Foreign Languages For Travelers site, at **http://www.travlang.com/languages/**. This site has pages covering 60 languages.

Say, for example, you want to listen to someone saying hello in Mandarin, the official language in China. From the home page, select *English* from the drop-down menu and click on the link to *Mandarin*. You will see a page of categories, including *Basic Words*, *Numbers*, and *Travel*. *Basic Words* should already be selected. Click on the *Submit* button to download a page containing a list of basic words. This list includes the Mandarin for hello, *Ni hao*. Click on the words to hear them being spoken.

Choose a language from this page.

Click on a word or phrase to hear it being pronounced.

32 USE WEB REFERENCE TOOLS

There is a large selection of reference tools, such as encyclopedias and dictionaries, on the Web. Once you get used to using them, you will be able to look up information quickly and easily.

A particularly useful site is the Research It! site at **http://www.itools.com/research-it/**. One of the things you can do on this site is find out about famous people. To do this, scroll down the home page to the *Biographical* section, which is listed under *Library Tools* and *People*. Type in the name of a person, for example the composer Mozart, and click on *look it up!* A page will download showing information about Mozart's life.

Other reference tools on the Research It! site include an online dictionary, a thesaurus and a rhyme finder.

The Research It! Web site includes several different reference tools.

A biography found using Research It!

There is a vast selection of computer games for Net users to sample and play. There are games you can download onto your computer and play by yourself, or you can join in online games with players all over the world.

33 DOWNLOAD A NEW GAME

A good site for finding games is GamesDomain's Web site at **http://www. gamesdomain.com/**. You will find both free games and games that you can buy. Many of the games that are for sale have free demonstration versions which you can download and try out before you decide to buy.

To find a game, click on *Downloads* on the home page. On the next page, click on the link to programs that will suit the operating system you have installed on your computer. For example, if you have *Windows 95*, select *Win 95*. A menu of different types of games will appear. Select *Newest 100* to see a list of new games. Click on one, and you will see more details about the game, and a list of sites from which you can download it. Select the nearest site to where you live, and the game will start to download.

Use projects 11 and 13 to help you download and install the game.

34 PLAY CHESS ONLINE

The Yahoo! Games site at **http://play. yahoo.com/** has a variety of different games that you can play online with other players. Select a game that you want to play from the home page, for example *Chess*. The first time you use

 Yahoo! Games, you need to register by completing an online form. To do this, click on *Get Registered* and follow the instructions.

Once you have registered, a menu will appear showing the different levels of chess you can play at, and the number of people currently playing in each level. Click on the level you want and you'll see a list of current games. Look for a game that only has one player and click on *Join* to play against them. When you see a window containing a game board, you can start the game.

You can also play Backgammon, Checkers, Cribbage and other games on the Yahoo! Games site.

Here are some of the games you will find on the Web. **Virtual Pool 2**

Sim City 2000 Network Edition

Monopoly

35 JOIN AN ONLINE ADVENTURE

You can enter a whole new world with role-playing games. Some of these games, such as *Magic: The Gathering*, can be played online. To use *Magic: The Gathering*, you will have to buy the program on CD-ROM. Visit its Web site at **http://www.gathering.net/**. If you decide to buy it, you can order the program from the MicroProse Online Store site, at **http://store.advaccess.com/microprose/**. To play the game online, you will also need a program called *ManaLink*, which you can download from the Net for free. (See

An image from the Magic: The Gathering Web site

project 49 for help with ordering items online, and page 93 for security information.)

Magic: The Gathering is based on a card game. Each player has a set of cards, which represent magic spells and can be used in the game. Players travel around a vast fantasy world, meeting characters who are playing the game at the same time. Playing the game online can take up a lot of time, which can be expensive. You can also play the game on your own off-line, going on quests and adventures.

Screen shots from Magic: The Gathering

A character in the game

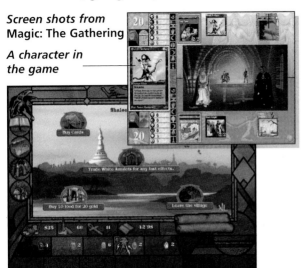

36 RACE CARS ON THE NET

There are games in which you can race cars against other competitors on the Net. Some of these games use amazing 3-D graphics to make it look like you're really in the driving seat.

Ultimate Race Pro is a 3-D race game. You can download a free demonstration version of the game from its Web site at **http://www.ultimaterace.com/**. From this page, follow the link to *Download*. Use projects 11 and 13 to download and install the demo. You may need to have an extra graphics card installed on your computer to play the game (see page 55).

The demonstration version of *Ultimate Race Pro* only allows you to play the game on your own. To play it online against other Net users, you'll need to buy the full version of the game on CD-ROM and set up an account to use it. You can order it from the MicroProse Online Store at **http://store.advaccess.com/microprose/**.

Scenes from games of Ultimate Race Pro

Movie buffs everywhere love the Internet, because it has a wealth of information about new and current films. There are hundreds of Web sites about movie stars set up by their fans. The Net is also a great source of gossip and news about films which are currently in production or about to be released.

A selection of movie-related Web sites

Men In Black at
http://www.meninblack.com/

(37) FIND FILMS IN YOUR AREA

You can use the Web to plan a trip to see a film. One site you may find useful is the Internet Movie Database. It contains a set of links to sites which show which films are showing in many different countries.

Visit the Web site at **http://us.imdb.com/Cinemas/**. Click on your country from the list which appears to see links to listings for your area. Simply click on the relevant link to find information about films on locally.

Space Jam at http://www.spacejam.com/

(38) MAKE YOUR OWN MOVIE ONLINE

The Interactive Simulation site at **http://library.advanced.org/10015/data/interact/sim/** lets you create an imaginary film and then tells you how it might have done at the box office.

To start creating a movie, click on *New Simulation* and follow the instructions on screen. You will have to select a password so that the site can save your simulation as you go along. This means you can stop working on it at any time, then return to it later.

Creating a movie involves making a lot of decisions. For example, you will be required to select an ending for the film and decide which shots to use when you are filming. There will always be several options you can choose from. Be careful to keep within your film's budget.

When you complete the film, the Web site will produce a page with a summary of how successful your imaginary film was.

This Web page asks you to choose a camera angle for your movie.

Some shots are more expensive to film than others.

Shot 7		
LEON: "Boy, I really hate dealing with people like this."		
$150,000	$200,000	$150,000

Click in a circle to select a shot.

39 SUBMIT A REVIEW

Why not tell other people about a film you've enjoyed watching by sending a review to a Web site? One site devoted to movie news and reviews is Popcorn at **http://www. hotpopcorn.com/**. This has a section where you can submit your own comments about films you've seen.

To submit a review, or any other comments, follow the link to *Email Sky!*, and fill in the online form on the page which appears. Check back at a later date to see whether your comments have been added to the *Readback the Feedback* page.

The Warner Brothers movie and TV site at
http://www.warnerbros.com/

Courtesy Warner Bros. Online

Independence Day at
http://www.id4movie.com/

40 WATCH A FILM PREVIEW

Most new film releases have their own Web sites. On some sites you can watch previews. Occasionally you can see a preview on the Web before it is shown elsewhere.

Start by finding a film's official Web site using the Internet Movie Database (IMDb) at **http://www.imdb.com/**. To find a Web site using IMDb, click on *SEARCH* on the home page. On the page which appears, type in the title of the film and click on *search*. Select the film you want from the list which appears. Click on the *Official* icon (shown here) and scroll down the page to find a link to the official site.

IMDb's Official icon

When you have downloaded a film's Web site, you may see a link on which you must click to watch a preview. The page that appears will display instructions about how to see the preview. Since previews are video clips, you will need a plug-in to view them (see pages 62-63).

The preview will be shown in a box in your browser window, or in a new window. You'll hear the soundtrack through your speakers or headphones.

Previews can take a long time to download, so be certain that you want to watch the one you've chosen before you begin to download it.

The Internet is used to exchange and publish data gathered by computers all over the world. So whether you want to study the annual rainfall in Australia or tomorrow's forecast for France, you'll find Web sites with detailed weather maps and information.

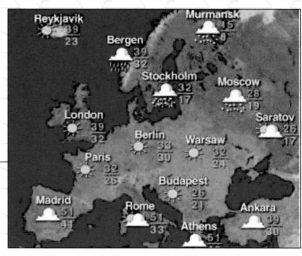

(41) PRINT OUT A WEATHER MAP

You can print out a map showing the weather for a country or a continent. One place to find weather maps is Yahoo! Weather, at **http://weather.yahoo.com/**. From its home page, click on the link to *Weather Maps*. Find your region on the grid, and click on *Outlook*. You will see a map showing the latest forecast.

You can print out any Web page exactly as you see it on screen, including all the words and pictures. To do this, select *Print* from the *File* menu while the page is displayed in your

A weather map from Yahoo! Weather

browser window. If you have to pay for the amount of time you spend connected to the Internet, it is a good idea to go off-line before you print out Web pages.

(42) CHECK THE WEATHER ON THIS DAY IN HISTORY

Can you remember what the weather was like on this day last year? Probably not; but you can find sites that have records of this information on the Web. The NCDC Climate Visualization Web site at **http://www.ncdc.**

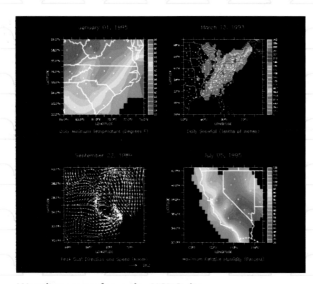

Weather maps from the NCDC site

noaa.gov/onlineprod/drought/xmgr.html has a collection of maps covering the United States of America that show weather information for any day, right back to 1893.

You can see up to four maps at once, each showing different information. From the home page, click on *Contour/Vectors*. Select the number of maps you want to see from the pull-down menu, and click on *Next*. On the next page, select a date for the first map. In the *Parameter* section, you can select daily maximum or minimum temperatures, rainfall, or snowfall. Scroll down and select the region you want to display.

When you have selected the information for all the maps, click on *Next*. You will see a confirmation screen. This tells you which maps you've selected. Check it and click on *Submit*.

The BBC Weather Centre at **http://www. bbc.co.uk/weather/** also has information about the weather on this day in history. To see this, click on *The Almanac* on the home page.

43 USE YOUR OWN WEATHER PROGRAM

To see up-to-date information about the weather all over the world on your computer's desktop, you can get a program called *WinWeather* from the Web.

The WinWeather *program displaying weather data*

City	Date	Temp	Hum.	Press.	Wind		Wthr	Fct
London	N/A	N/A	N/A	N/A	N/A		N/A	N/A
New York	20 Jan 1998 09:51 AM EST	+35°	69%	29.98		9 WNW		ⓘ
San Francisco	N/A	N/A	N/A	N/A	N/A		N/A	N/A
Los Angeles	N/A	N/A	N/A	N/A	N/A		N/A	N/A
San Francisco	20 Jan 1998 06:56 AM PST	+46°	89%	30.03	NORTH	0	scattered clouds	ⓘ
Los Angeles	20 Jan 1998 06:50 AM PST	+51°	71%	29.93		4		ⓘ
London	1PM JAN 20 1998	+41°	N/A	N/A	N/A			N/A

Temperature ——————┘   **This symbol indicates that the weather is cloudy.**

To download a free 30-day trial version of *WinWeather*, visit the Insanely Great Software Web site at **http://www.igsnet.com/**. Follow the *WinWeather* link from the home page to download the program. (See projects 11 and 13 for help with downloading and installing it.)

When you start *WinWeather* and go online, you will see a window showing the weather in different cities. The program will take a few minutes to collect current information. You can change the choice of cities by going to the *Configure* menu and selecting *Configure Cities*. A menu of cities to choose from will appear.

WinWeather also features direct access to weather Web cameras (see project 85). To see live weather pictures, select *International Cams* from the *Images* menu, and choose a camera to look through.

44 JOIN A WEATHER PROJECT

You can get involved in a project studying and comparing the weather with Net users in other countries on the One Sky, Many Voices site at **http://onesky.engin.umich.edu/**. Click on the name of one of the projects to find out all about it.

To register for a project, click on *REGISTER* on the home page, and fill in the online form which appears. Click on *Submit* and you will be sent an e-mail containing full instructions.

One Sky, Many Voices organizes weather-based projects for students all over the world.

You can find lots of weather pictures like these on the Australian Severe Weather site at http://australian severeweather. simplenet.com/

Dinosaurs may be extinct on Earth, but they're still thriving on the Internet. Many museums have online dinosaur exhibitions where you can learn about prehistoric life. Other sites enable you to test your knowledge. There are plenty of dinosaur pictures to look at on the Web and you can even watch dinosaurs coming back to life on your screen.

45 VISIT A DINOSAUR MUSEUM

One way to learn about dinosaurs is by touring an online museum, such as the Hunterian Museum. The museum's entrance hall is at **http://www.gla.ac.uk/Museum/ tour/entrance/**.

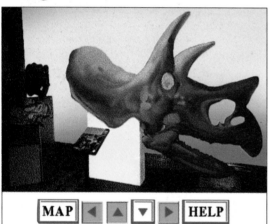

Take an online tour at the Hunterian Museum.

From the entrance hall, use the direction buttons to explore the museum. To see a plan of the museum, click on *Map*. You can go directly to any of the rooms by clicking on the appropriate part of the map. Once you are in an exhibition room, you can click on some of the exhibits to find out more about them.

46 EXPLORE A FILM WEB SITE

Many Web sites have behind-the-scenes information about how films are made. For example, you'll find out fascinating facts about how the special effects in the dinosaur movie *The Lost World* were achieved by visiting its Web site at **http://www.lost-world.com/**. To access the main site, click on the picture on the Web page which appears. From the Web page showing an office, you can explore the site by clicking on the map which is shown hanging on a wall.

Follow the link to *Site B* to get technical secrets from the film. The Web site is split into several areas, each one with different information. Try clicking on *Hunter's Camp* to see how the dinosaurs were animated, and how scenes were filmed.

Dinosaur pictures from Dinosauria at http://www.dinosauria.com/

47   DOWNLOAD A DINOSAUR SCREEN SAVER

The Web offers a vast selection of animated screen savers which you can install on your computer. To find a screen saver with dinosaurs on it, search the Web using **+dinosaur +"screen saver"** (see project 6). A list of links will appear. Follow a link to find information about a dinosaur screen saver.

Click on a screen saver's link to download it. In the window which appears, select your browser's *Download* folder as the destination of your screen saver. Unzip your screen saver using the instructions given in project 13, and place it in your *Windows/System* folder.

To activate the screen saver, go offline and click on your *Start* button. Select *Settings* and *Control Panel*. Double-click on the *Display* icon. Select the *Screen Saver* tab from the *Display Properties* window. Click on the *Screen Saver* pull-down menu to see a list of your system's screen savers. There are normally several to choose from.

Click on the name of the dinosaur screen saver, and then click *OK* to activate it. You can set the exact length of time for the computer to wait before it displays the screen saver in the *Wait* box.

The screen saver pull-down menu

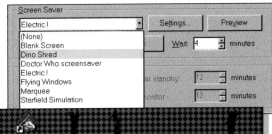

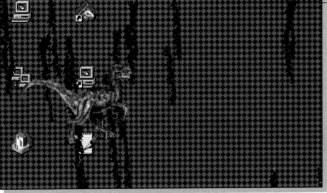

This screen saver is of a dinosaur which appears to tear up the desktop.

48   DO A DINOSAUR QUIZ

Test your dinosaur knowledge by doing a quiz on the Web. The Question Mark site has a good one at **http://www.questionmark. com/qmwebquestions/dino2.htm**.

This page contains a list of questions with multiple choice answers. To select an answer to a question, click in the circle next to your choice. You may have to answer some questions by typing an answer into a box. When you've finished, click on the button at the bottom of the screen to find out the correct answers. You will also see your answers, and your score.

The Web gives you access to all kinds of pieces of writing, from poems to academic articles, and novels to teen magazines. You can read texts online or place an order for a paper version.

There are Web sites where you can have your own work published and on-going writing projects to join in.

(49) SHOP AT AN INTERNET BOOKSTORE

Internet bookstores are Web sites which sell books. Their main advantage is that they can offer millions of titles, far more than you'll find in any store. They also feature articles about new books and authors, comments from readers, and recommendations.

One Internet bookstore is Amazon.com, at **http://www.amazon.com/**. To look at the books available to buy, use the search facility on its home page, or click on *Browse Subjects*. The site also has information on new books.

At Amazon.com, like many Internet shopping sites, you can use a device known as a shopping cart in which you gather all the books you want to buy. To place a book in the cart, click on the *Add it to your Shopping Cart* button.

To pay for the books you have chosen, you have to complete an online form. You will need to give the address where you want the books delivered and state how you are going to pay for them. Most people who buy things via the Web pay for their goods with a credit card. (To buy things online you need to be over 18. If you're not, ask someone who is to help you.) To find more information about shopping on the Net see pages 92-93

A selection of Internet bookstores

http://www.okukbooks.com/

http://www.amazon.com/

http://www.barnesandnoble.com/

50) GET A POEM PUBLISHED ONLINE

Writers all over the world have had their stories and poems published on the Web.

One site that encourages Net users to submit work for publication is Positively Poetry at **http://advicom.net/~e-media/kv/poetry1.html**. To send your own poem, follow the *Submit* link from the home page and enter your poem onto the online form.

Alternatively, you can send in your poem by e-mail. Make sure you read the site's rules for submitting poems. One such rule is that the poem must not be over 25 lines in length. The site organizers choose poems to go on the site, and remove old ones after three months. The site always contains lots of poems to read.

51) ADD TO A NEVERENDING STORY

Some of the stories you'll find on the Web have been written jointly by a large number of people. They are called neverending stories. A neverending story starts when someone publishes the beginning of a story on a Web site and invites other people to send in contributions to continue the plot. These sections are put straight onto the Web, so that Net users can follow the story as it develops.

A good place to read a neverending story is the Kidpub site at **http://www.kidpub.org/kidpub/**. It has a different story each week. Click on the title of the neverending story on the home page to read this week's story.

To add to the story, click on the link at the bottom of the page and complete the online form that appears. You'll receive an e-mail explaining how to contribute. Anything you submit will be added to the story immediately.

Kidpub's home page

52) FIND A BOOK ONLINE

Many famous works of literature are published on the Net. The Internet Public Library at **http://www.ipl.org/** has links to over 5,000 books which are stored on Internet computers.

To help you find a particular play, poem or novel, this site includes a search engine. Say, for

The Internet Public Library home page

example, you want to find one of Shakespeare's sonnets. Click on *Online Texts* on the Internet Public Library home page. You will see a search page. Type **Shakespeare Sonnets** into the box and click on *Search*. You'll see a list of links to online versions of a book called *The Sonnets*.

Click on one of these links to download the book. This may take a few minutes. Then scroll down the page to find the sonnet you want to read. You could also print out the page (see project 41).

The Internet is fast becoming one of the most popular places to find the latest news. Search services and newspapers have Web sites on which stories appear almost as they happen.

Newspaper Web sites from all over the world

http://www. lemonde.fr/

(53) GET THE LATEST NEWS

You can make sure that up-to-date news is sent to your computer automatically. To do this you will need a browser which uses "Push" channels. A Push channel is a window within your browser which, while you are online, continually gathers specific information for you, such as news stories or TV schedules.

http://www. usatoday.com/

Netscape Communicator 4, *Microsoft Internet Explorer 4*, or a later version of either browser, can include Push channels. *Netscape Communicator's* Push channel program is called *Netcaster* (find out more at **http://www. netscape.com/**). *Microsoft Internet Explorer* uses a program called *Webcaster* (see **http:// www.microsoft.com/**).

To start up *Netcaster*, select its name in *Netscape's Communicator* menu. To use *Webcaster*, click on *Internet Explorer's Channels* button. Your browser will guide you through the process of setting up a channel so you can get up-to-date information while you're online.

http://www.press.co.nz/

(54) WRITE FOR A MAGAZINE

Why not contribute to a Web magazine that is created by people all over the world? Kidlink, at **http://www.kidlink.org/KIDPROJ/ Magazine/**, organizes a Web magazine. The articles it contains are written by young people from many different countries.

To take part in the magazine project yourself, you need to join its mailing list (see project 25). Send an e-mail to **listserv@listserv.**

Kidlink's home page

nodak.edu with the message *subscribe KIDPROJ* and your name. You will be sent more information about the magazine and the kind of articles you can write for it.

The BBC Online Push channel in Internet Explorer

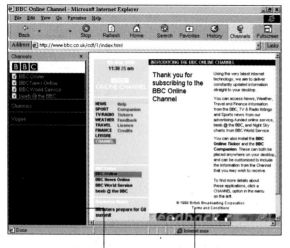

List of available channels   *BBC Online channel*

55 CREATE AN ONLINE NEWSPAPER

You can select the information you want to read by creating your own online newspaper. Crayon's Web site at **http://www. crayon.net/** creates your own set of links to news sites. You can use it each day to get the type of news that interests you.

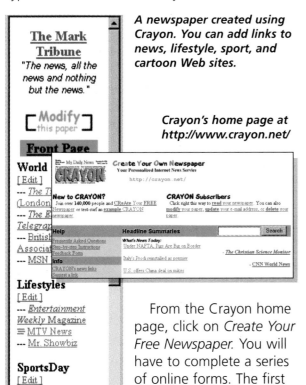

A newspaper created using Crayon. You can add links to news, lifestyle, sport, and cartoon Web sites.

Crayon's home page at http://www.crayon.net/

From the Crayon home page, click on *Create Your Free Newspaper*. You will have to complete a series of online forms. The first form asks you to enter your e-mail address and choose a password. The other forms ask you to choose exactly what you want your newspaper to look like and which news sites you want it to link to. For example, you can choose a title, motto and layout for your newspaper.

When you have finished, click on *Publish My Newspaper*. You will be shown the URL of the Web page on which your newspaper will appear. As your newspaper is personal, its URL includes your e-mail address so that other people cannot read it or find it by accident. The URL will be quite long so it's a good idea to create a short cut to it (see project 2).

56 WORK WITH THE NEWS

You may find a news story on the Web which is relevant to a piece of work you're doing. It's easy to copy text from a Web page into a word processing program and insert it into an essay or project. First save all the text on the Web page by selecting *Save As* from the *File* menu. In the *Save as type* box, select *Plain text*, and change the ending of the file name from *.html* to *.txt*. Click on *OK* to save the file.

Go offline, close your browser, and open a word processing program. Select *File* and *Open*, and browse to find the document you saved. You will see the text from the Web page. You can change how the text looks and you can copy a section of text to use as a quote by highlighting it and using the *Copy* and *Paste* commands in your word processing program's *Edit* menu.

If you copy text from a Web site in this way, ensure that you make it clear that it is not your own work. You should also state where you found the information.

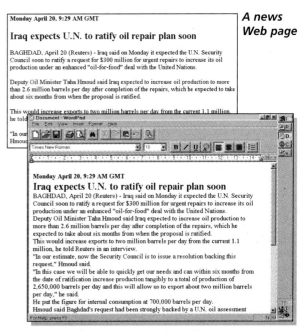

A news Web page

The text from the page above has been copied into a word processing program.

The Internet gives you access to millions of recipes for dishes from all over the world. There is also plenty of information about healthy eating. Many companies use the Net to publicize food products, and you can sometimes buy meals online.

You can find out how to make these dishes at http:// www.ilovepasta.org/

(57) FIND A RECIPE ON THE WEB

You can find the recipe for a specific dish by searching the Web using the names of its main ingredients. This is also a good way to find out what you could make with any ingredients you already have at home.

Gourmet World's site has information about food and cooking.

For example, a search using the words **+recipe +chicken +mushrooms** would give you a list of recipes including chicken and mushroom pie, and chicken casserole.

Gourmet World, at **http://www.gourmet world.com/**, has links to a wide range of recipes, information about restaurants, links to online food shops, and food facts. To find a recipe, click on *Culinary Center* on the home page, and select *Gourmet World Cookbook* from the page which appears. Next, select a category of food, such as *Casseroles*. A list of links to recipes will appear. Click on a link to see a recipe. If it sounds appetizing, you can print it out (see project 41) so that you can make it yourself.

(58) ORDER FOOD ONLINE

To order a meal online, you have to find a local restaurant which offers an online order service. You place your order by filling in an online form. The food is delivered to your home when it is ready.

You could search by key word (see project 3) to find sites which offer this service. Use the type of food you want, the word **online**, and the name of your town, as key words. A search using **+pizza +online +London**, for example, will produce a list of results showing pizza restaurants in London which take online orders.

Pizza Online at http://www.pizzaonline.com/ has links to restaurants in the USA and Canada which accept online orders.

59 CREATE A VIRTUAL PIZZA

Imagine a pizza with sinks, footballs, and smiling faces as toppings. It may not sound very appetizing, but there is a Web site where you can create a virtual pizza with all kinds of strange ingredients. The Internet Pizza Server is at **http://www.ecst.csuchico.edu/~pizza/**.

To design a pizza, scroll down the home page, and click on the link to *Order and view a pizza over the Web*. You will see an online form that lists a variety of ingredients. To select a topping, place a mark in the box next to it. You could be conventional and choose olives, ground beef and green peppers. Alternatively, you could choose more unusual ingredients, such as beetles, road signs and kittens. You can create a truly bizarre combination on your virtual pizza.

When you've finished, click on *order pizza* to download your pizza. A page containing a picture of the pizza will appear on your screen.

60 GET RECIPES BY E-MAIL

You can get a regular supply of recipes by joining a mailing list (see project 25). Mm-recipes runs a list which sends out recipes, and lets its members respond to requests for recipes from other people. You will normally receive between 10 and 20 messages from the list each day, including recipes and cooking advice. To join, send an e-mail to **majordomo @idiscover.net** with the message *subscribe mm-recipes* (see project 8). You will be sent an e-mail containing instructions on how to use the mailing list.

This virtual pizza has beetles, nails, olives, salami and road signs on top.

61 PUT YOUR RECIPE ON THE WEB

Some Web sites encourage you to contribute your own recipes, which are then put on the site. CyberRecipes, at **http://www. cyberpages.com/recipe**, has a large collection of recipes arranged by the country they're from.

To add a recipe to the site, follow the link to *Please add your own recipe!* Fill in the online form, including your country, the title of the recipe, the ingredients, and the preparation instructions, and click on *Add This!*

Your recipe will be added to the Web site. You can see it by following the link from the home page to the initial letter of your country, and scrolling down the page to your recipe.

If you put a recipe on the Web, make sure that it's worded carefully, so that people can follow it successfully.

The Net is invaluable if you are planning a trip. You can use it to book tickets and get tourist information. There are thousands of Web sites which will tell you about countries, and suggest places to visit and things to see.

Alternatively, you can make a "virtual" journey, visiting sites across the world and even sending postcards without actually leaving your computer.

A Swiss travel gallery Web site

The Land of Beauty

Series One: Top Ten Scenic Sites

A gallery of travel pictures from China

The Jamaican Tourist Board Web site at http://www.jamaicatravel.com/

63 GET AN AIRLINE TIMETABLE

You can find timetables for planes and trains all over the world on the Web. One company which has online timetables is Air France, which operates flights all over the world. You can find a timetable at **http://www.airfrance.com/**.

To see a timetable, click on *Schedules* on the home page. A page will download with an online form. Fill in the departure city, destination, and date of travel, and click on *Submit*. A page showing a timetable of flights will appear.

62 FIND TRAVEL PICTURES

To get ideas for amazing places to visit, you can look at other people's travel pictures on the Web. Use a search service that specializes in locating images, such as Image Surfer at **http://isurf.yahoo.com/**.

To find travel pictures, follow the link to *Recreation* from the Image Surfer home page. On the next page, scroll down to *Travel*, and select a location, such as *Hawaii*. You will see a set of thumbnail pictures. These are linked to Web pages which may have more pictures.

64 FIND TOURIST INFORMATION

You can use the Web to get information about tourism in almost any country. One good way to find a range of information about travel to a country is to use Excite Travel at **http://city.net/**.

Say, for example, you wanted to find some information about Jamaica. From Excite Travel's home page, click on *Caribbean* on the map. A page with a map of the Caribbean will download. Click on *Jamaica* to see a list of links to sites relating to tourism there.

65 SEND AN E-MAIL POSTCARD

Use the Net to find postcards which you can e-mail to friends. The E-Cards Web site at **http://www.e-cards.com/** has a wide selection of designs to choose from.

To send a postcard, go to the home page and click on *Write & Send*. You'll see a list of the different categories into which the postcards are divided. For postcards of places, click on *Region Selector.* A page showing a world map will download. Click on the part of the world you want your card to show.

The next page contains a set of thumbnail images of the postcards you could send. Click on one to select it.

The card will appear on your screen with an online form. Write a message and fill in the recipient's e-mail address, and your own. When you've finished, click on the link to *Build & Preview this card!*.

When you send a postcard, it's not delivered directly to the recipient's e-mail address, but is stored at its own Web address. The recipient will be sent an e-mail saying that there is a postcard waiting at that address. The e-mail will also contain instructions on how to look at the card.

This e-card shows a picture from Indonesia.

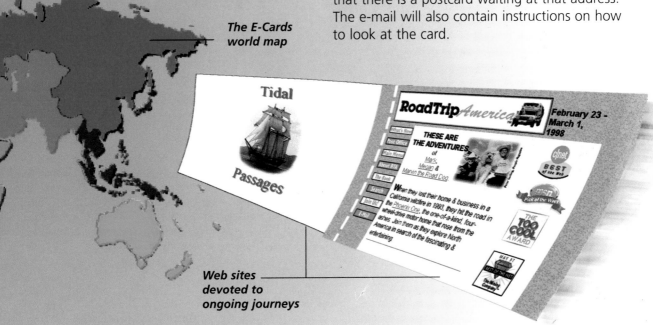

The E-Cards world map

Web sites devoted to ongoing journeys

66 FOLLOW A WEB JOURNEY

Some people set up Web sites so they can report their journeys as they make them. You can see where they've been, and find out what their travel plans are. Sometimes the sites are updated every day. Their creators use lap-top computers and connect to the Web by satellite phone to do this. Sites can be created from ships, cars or even planes.

One such site is the Road Trip America Web site, at **http://www.RoadTripAmerica.com/ index.html**. You can follow the adventures of a family which is driving around the USA in a mobile home. From the home page, see the latest bulletin from the family by clicking on *What's New*. You will see a page about the places they've visited recently.

The Net makes it possible to chat to other people who are online. You can make new friends across the world, or keep in contact with people you already know who are a long way away. Some Net users make arrangements to be online at specific times, so that people can find them and chat to them regularly.

67 USE AN INTERNET PHONE

You can use the Net to talk to people, just like using a telephone. To do this you will need some Internet telephone software, speakers and a microphone you can connect your computer. When you have installed the software, you can talk to people in other countries without having to pay long-distance call charges. You only have to pay for a local telephone call to your Internet access provider.

Find out about using an Internet phone on the VocalTec site at **http://www.vocaltec.com/**. This site also has software which you can download to start using a Net phone (see project 11).

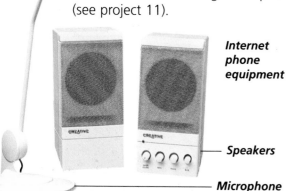

Internet phone equipment

— *Speakers*

— *Microphone*

SAFE CHATTING

• Don't continue talking to people who say things that you don't like.
• Be aware that people can pretend to be whoever they like when they chat online.
• Don't spend too much time chatting, as time spent online costs money.

68 CHAT TO PEOPLE OVER THE NET

One of the most well-established forms of online chat is Internet Relay Chat, or IRC. You need an IRC program to take part in this. With IRC, people chat to each other in groups called channels. Each channel has a title which covers the main interest of the group, such as *Teen* for teenage users.

A chat session in a program called mIRC

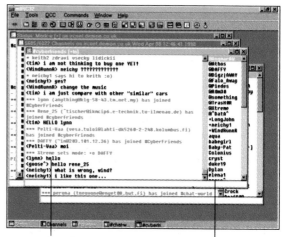

This window shows an ongoing chat.

List of people chatting

During a chat session you will see text written by other users appearing on your screen. To say something yourself, simply type it in and press *Return*. It will appear on your screen, and on the screens of all the other users, immediately. Other people can respond and start up conversations with you.

There are a number of IRC programs available free for a trial period. You can download one called *mIRC* from **http://www.mirc.co.uk/**. For help with downloading programs, see project 11. The mIRC Web site contains full instructions on how to install the program on your computer. You'll find more information in the *Help* files provided with *mIRC*. IRC is quite complicated to use, so you may want to print out the information in the *Help* files.

69) VISIT A VIRTUAL WORLD

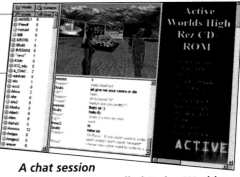

On the Net you will find sites which contain amazing 3-D environments. These places, called virtual worlds, are created with Virtual Reality (VR). VR is the use of computers to create objects and places which appear to be real.

There are several types of virtual worlds which you can visit, including dungeons, landscapes and palaces. In some virtual worlds, known as 3-D chat rooms, you can chat to other people who are visiting that particular world at the same time as you.

To use a virtual world, you'll need to download a program from the Net.

A chat session using a program called **Active Worlds**

Avatars talking in **Active Worlds**

You can download a trial version of a VR program called *Onlive! Traveler* for free from **http://www.onlive. com/prod/trav/**. See project 11 for help with downloading programs.

Before you enter a virtual world, you have to choose an "avatar". This is a character which will represent you in the virtual world. It may look like a person, an animal or an alien. You use your arrow keys or your mouse to instruct your avatar to move.

When you come across avatars representing other people, you can start chatting. In some virtual worlds, you use your keyboard to type in what you want to say to the people you meet. In others, you can actually hear what people are saying and talk to them using a microphone.

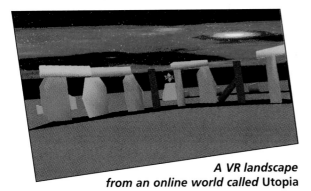

A VR landscape from an online world called **Utopia**

70) HAVE A VIDEOCONFERENCE

A videoconference is a telephone conversation where you can see the person you're talking to.

You can use the Internet to have a videoconference. To do this, you will need a microphone, some speakers and a type of camera that you can attach to your computer, such as the Intel Internet Video Phone.

You will also need some software. The most popular program is *CU-SeeMe*. You can download a free version of this from the *CU-SeeMe* site at **http://cu-seeme.cornell.edu/**.

The **CU-SeeMe** *Web site* ———

When you go online and make a call, you will see the person you're talking to in a window on your screen, and hear them speak through your speakers. The person you are contacting will need to have the same hardware and software as you.

A video phone conversation

You can go shopping for almost anything using the Internet. Whether you want to buy clothes, gifts, or CDs, you'll find a wide range available through the Web. Many stores operate solely on the Web; they don't have any other branches. Others use the Web to promote or advertize their products and services.

71 VISIT A SHOPPING MALL

An online shopping mall is a site which brings together several Web shopping sites. You can access lots of stores from one site, just as you can at a real shopping mall.

The Internet Mall, for example, at **http://www.shopnow.com/**, has links to over 25,000 stores. You can use the search facility on the home page to find what you are looking for. Type a keyword into the box, select the section you want to search, and click on the *Search* button to download a list of links to shops. For example, to find stores selling cameras, search using the word **camera** in *The Technology Center*. Projects 49 and 72 explain how to pay for things online.

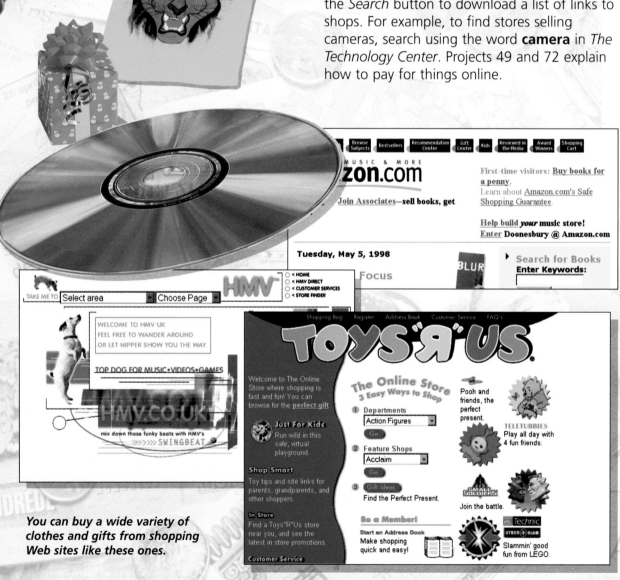

You can buy a wide variety of clothes and gifts from shopping Web sites like these ones.

72 USE ONLINE CASH

Some people pay for things that they buy on the Net with online cash. This is also called electronic cash, or eCash™. It has the same value as ordinary paper or metal money, but is actually data stored on a computer. The data can be used as money when it is transferred from one computer to another.

To use eCash, you have to withdraw it from your bank account using the Internet, and store it on your computer's hard disk. Search the Web for your bank's Web site and visit it to find out if your bank offers an eCash service. If it does, its site will have full instructions on how to set up the facility on your computer.

You can find out more about using eCash at the Digicash®Web site, at **http://www.digicash.com/**.

You can pay for things using an eCash™ purse, when the system is set up on your machine.

73 GUESS A WEB ADDRESS

Many companies have Web sites from which you can buy their products directly. If you don't already know the URL of a company's Web site, you can often guess it. Try typing in the company's name and adding *www.* before it and *.com* after it. For example you will find Nike at **http://www.nike.com/**.

© 1998 Mattel

Try to guess the URLs for the Barbie Web site and the Reebok Web site.

SECURITY

When you pay for things online, make sure the site you use is using a "secure" server. This means that information sent to the site, including addresses and credit card details, cannot be seen by anyone else. The information is turned into a code when it is sent across the Net, and changed back when it is received.

If you visit a secure server, your browser will display an unbroken key symbol, or a locked padlock. This usually appears in the bottom left corner of the browser window.

SHOPPING TIPS

• Always check whether an item you are buying can be delivered to the country you live in, as this is not always possible.
• Make sure the item you buy is exactly what you want, and that you can return it if you change your mind.
• To buy things online you need to be over 18. If you're not, ask an adult to help you.
• Some companies like to send e-mails to customers to give them news about their sites. There is usually a box on a company's order form you can place a mark in if you don't want to receive these e-mails.

The Internet brings together people from all over the world. This makes it a great place to learn about world environmental issues and to discover what you can do to help.

74 CHECK THE SMOG LEVEL IN L.A.

Cities throughout the world are falling victim to air pollution caused by traffic and factories. Los Angeles, California, is notorious for this kind of pollution, known as smog. Organizations there have pioneered the measurement and forecasting of air pollution.

You can check the current smog level in L.A. by visiting the Air Quality Management District page at **http://www.aqmd.gov/**. Click on the lung icon to see today's smog readings, and the forecast for tomorrow.

75 EXPLORE A GREEN CITY

A good Web site for information about how to live a greener life is Recycle City's site, at **http://www.epa.gov/recyclecity/**. The site contains an imaginary environmentally-friendly city. Each part of the city has information about a different aspect of green living so you can learn as you explore.

From the home page, click on *Go to Recycle City!* to see the map shown here.

76 SEE A PANORAMIC SCENE

You can look around a natural scene using the *Quicktime* plug-in. Download and install it from **http://www.apple.com/quicktime/** using projects 11, 12 and 13.

One place you can find a panoramic nature scene (a scene you can move around in and look at different views) is at **http://www.research.digital.com/PA/maps/parks-content.html**. Click on *Gallery* and choose a view from the page which appears. Wait for the picture to appear, and drag your cursor across it to look left or right.

A panoramic nature scene

You can explore the city by clicking on the map. For example, if you click on the bottom right corner, you'll see a close-up of that part of town. Click on a building, such as the factory, to see inside. You'll discover objects you can click on, such as a pile of paper in the factory, to discover how the city has been made greener.

A map of Recycle City

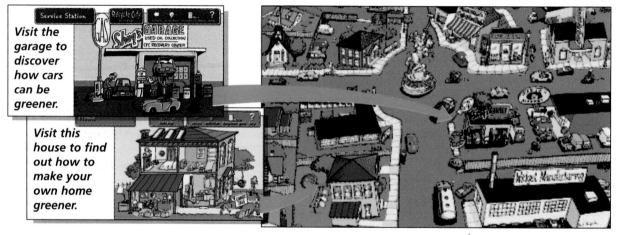

Visit the garage to discover how cars can be greener.

Visit this house to find out how to make your own home greener.

(77) EXPLORE A WORLD GREEN GROUP

Groups all over the world have Web sites devoted to the environment. Some international organizations and companies maintain central sites which link to local sites in different countries. One example is the Greenpeace site. You'll find it at **http://www.greenpeace.org/**.

Use the central Greenpeace site to find one of the national branches of the organization. On the home page, click on the link to *National Offices*. You will see a page with a set of flags which link to the different branches. Choose a country and click on its flag to visit the local Greenpeace site. On some countries' sites you can join Greenpeace online.

Greenpeace International

Use the links page to visit different branches.

Greenpeace UK

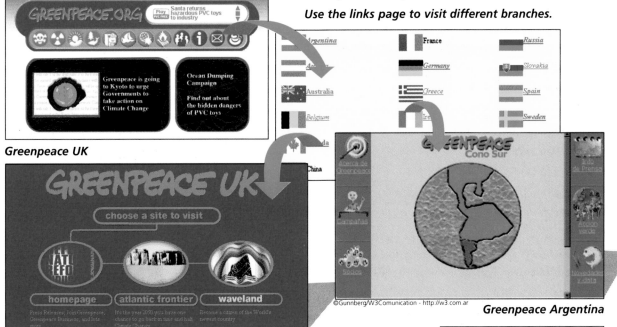

©Gunnberg/W3Comunication - http://w3.com.ar

Greenpeace Argentina

(78) TRANSLATE A WEB PAGE

If any of the sites you want to visit are in other languages, you can use the AltaVista Translator site at **http://babelfish.altavista.digital.com/** to translate them.

Say, for example, you want to translate the Greenpeace Italy site at **http://www.greenpeace.it/** into English. On the AltaVista Translator home page, click on the form and type in Greenpeace Italy's URL. Select the languages you want to translate from and to, *Italian to English*, using the drop-down list. Finally, click on the *Translate* button. A translated version of the page will download.

Use the AltaVista Translator form to translate a Web page.

Sometimes a message will appear saying that the AltaVista Translator site can't translate a page. There may be too much text, or the page may have a slow Net connection. If you see this message, highlight the text you want to read on the original page, and select *Copy* from the *Edit* menu. On the translator page, click on the form and select *Paste* from the *Edit* menu. Select the languages and press *Translate*. You should see a translation of the text you highlighted.

You may never have seen a ghost or a UFO, but you'll find plenty of people on the Net who claim that they have. You can judge for yourself whether pictures of the yeti or the Loch Ness Monster posted on the Web are genuine. You can also find people who claim that they have been abducted by aliens or haunted by poltergeists. Almost every strange theory about the paranormal has its own Web site, and every bizarre sighting or investigation is thoroughly reported and discussed.

79 REPORT A UFO SIGHTING

Anyone who thinks they may have spotted an unidentified flying object (UFO) can report their sighting directly to professional investigators via the Net. Many UFO research organizations have sites on the Web. For example, the International Society For UFO Research (ISUR) has a Web site at **http://www.isur.com/**.

On this site you will find an archive of past UFO sightings and an online form which people can use to report the details of a new sighting. To see this online form, click on *Report a Sighting* on the home page. To explore the archive, follow the *UFO Archive* link.

A picture of a UFO from ISUR's Web site

80 EXPLAIN CROP CIRCLES

Crop circles are strange mathematical shapes which have appeared mysteriously in fields all over the world. Although some have been proved to be hoaxes, scientists remain baffled about many others.

You can find some of the different explanations for crop circles on the Web. A good source of information on all kinds of unexplained phenomena is the Fortean Times site at **http://www.forteantimes.com/**. This is an "e-zine" (an electronic version of a printed magazine). It contains articles from the printed version, as well as extra features.

To read an article, go to the home page and select *articles*, and then *full article index*. A list of articles will download. Click on an article to read it.

The Fortean Times site has articles about crop circles.

Crop circle pictures posted on the Web

81 SEE A GHOST?

You can visit a Web site which is on the lookout for ghosts. The GhostWatcher, at **http://www.flyvision.org/sitelite/Houston/ GhostWatcher/**, is run by a woman named June Houston, who believes her house is haunted. She has placed Web cameras (see project 85) throughout her house, so that visitors to the site can report anything suspicious to her.

To look around the house, go to the Ghostwatcher home page. Click on a location where cameras have been set up, for example there are a collection of cameras in June's basement. Select a camera to look through, and your browser will download an up-to-date picture of that area. If you do see anything unusual, fill in the online form under the picture and click on *Send your Report*.

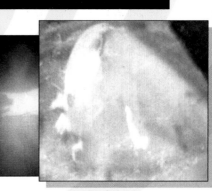

The GhostWatcher home page

These pictures, from the Ghost Web site at http://www. ghostweb.com/, allegedly show genuine ghosts.

82 DOWNLOAD AN ALIEN CURSOR

Get aliens to invade your desktop by replacing your mouse pointers with moving pictures known as animated cursors. A lot of Web sites have animated cursors which you can download. To use animated cursors, you need *Windows 95*.

There is a good selection of alien cursors at **http://www.parkave.net/users/fitz/**. Download and unzip a few using projects 11 and 13. Put them into your *Cursors* folder, which is in the *Windows* directory on your C drive.

To change the appearance of a particular pointer, go to *Settings* in the *Start* menu and select *Control Panel*. In the next window, double-click on *Mouse* to see the *Mouse Properties* window. Use the *Pointers* sheet to

select a pointer to change, for example, the *Busy* pointer, then click *Browse...*. Select one of the cursors you downloaded from the list in the *Browse* window, and click *OK*. The next time your computer is busy, you'll see an animated alien instead of the hour glass pointer.

Using the Browse *window* to select a new cursor

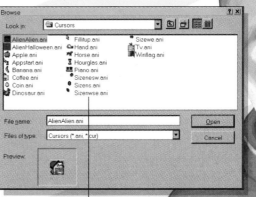

Your desktop could be invaded by aliens like these.

Animated cursor files

You can get close to earthquakes, volcanoes and hurricanes safely by using your computer. The Internet gives you access to pictures and film clips of natural disasters. You can also follow the latest news about events as they happen.

83 EXPLORE AN EARTHQUAKE SITE

In 1995, an earthquake devastated the Japanese city of Kobe. Over 4,000 people were killed, and around 120,000 houses were damaged or destroyed.

To see the chaos caused by the earthquake, go to the Kobe City Web site at **http://www. kobe-cufs.ac.jp/kobe-city/quake/ index.html**. Click on the *The Archives of 1995-1996* link to see a list of pictures taken of the city on different dates throughout that year.

Since the disaster, Kobe has gradually been rebuilt. To see how the rebuilding process was progressing two years after the disaster, use your browser's *Back* button to return to the site's home page. Click on *The Archives of 1997* link. On the page which appears, click on *A Pictorial News Brief*. You will see a page with thumbnail images of new and rebuilt buildings.

The Kobe site is regularly updated. You might like to create a short cut to it so you can check up on how rebuilding work is progressing. You can find out how to do this in project 2.

Pictures from the Web which show how Kobe has recovered since the earthquake

84 TRACK THE PATH OF A HURRICANE

On the Web you can follow the paths of tropical storms and hurricanes. One site which has maps that show the movement of hurricanes is The Hurricane & Storm Tracking Web site at **http://hurricane.terrapin.com/**.

This site uses programs called Java™ applets to show images of moving storms. Java is a programming language which is used to make pictures on Web pages move, or change, when you click on them. To see Java applets, you will need *Netscape Navigator 3.0*, *Internet Explorer 3.0*, or a later version of either browser.

To watch the movement of a storm that took place in 1997, follow the link to *Hurricane Plots and Data 1886-1997*, select *1997* from the drop-down list of years, and click on the name of a storm. A map will download showing where the storm occurred. Click on it to follow the path of the storm.

Satellite pictures of tropical storms from the Earth Science Enterprise site at http://www.hq.nasa.gov/office/ese/gallery/

85 SEE LIVE VOLCANO PICTURES

Pictures from the Cascades Volcano Observatory site at http://vulcan.wr.usgs.gov/home.html

You can look through devices called Web cameras to watch events as they occur across the world. Web cameras are attached to computers and transmit pictures to Web sites. The pictures are updated at regular intervals.

You can actually use a Web camera to try to see a live volcano. One site where you can do this is at **http://www.actrix.gen.nz/ruapehu/**. It contains pictures taken by a Web camera located near a volcano called Mount Ruapehu in New Zealand.

When Mount Ruapehu is inactive, the camera does not broadcast current pictures. If this is the case, click on the *Best pictures & movies* link to view pictures of the last big eruption. To see a film clip you will need the *Quicktime* plug-in. (For information about downloading plug-ins see project 11.)

Using the Web is a great way to visit museums and galleries all over the world. You can copy famous paintings onto your computer or publish your own works of art.

86 VISIT AN INTERACTIVE EXHIBIT

You can explore the exhibits on display in a museum by visiting its Web site. A good place to try is the Exploratorium site at **http://www.exploratorium.edu/**.

The Exploratorium home page

To see an exhibit, click on *Digital Library* on the home page. From the page which appears, select *Electronic Exhibits*. A list of links will appear. Click on one to download an exhibit.

The exhibit shown below studies how people remember faces. The faces of three famous people have been pasted onto a picture of Elvis.

People visiting the exhibit are asked to guess the identity of these famous faces.

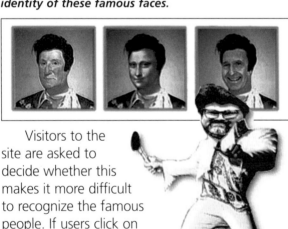

Visitors to the site are asked to decide whether this makes it more difficult to recognize the famous people. If users click on one of the pictures they can find out whose face was used to create it.

A cartoon from the Exploratorium Web site

87 GET SOME ART WALLPAPER

As you explore museums and galleries online, you may come across a picture you particularly like. You could use this to decorate your desktop. A layer of patterns or pictures that covers your desktop is called wallpaper.

To use a picture from the Web as your wallpaper, wait until the picture has completely downloaded, then click on it with your right mouse button. From the menu which appears, select *Set As Wallpaper*. When you close your browser, and any other programs you have open, you will see the picture on your desktop. Depending on how your computer is set up, the picture will either appear in the middle of your desktop, or in a repeated pattern like tiles on a wall.

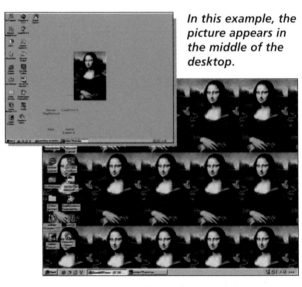

In this example, the picture appears in the middle of the desktop.

In this example, the picture has been tiled.

You can change the way the picture is displayed. To do this in *Windows 95*, go to the *Start* menu and select *Settings*, then *Control Panel*. Double-click on the *Display* icon in the *Control Panel* window. The *Display Properties* dialog box will appear. On the *Background* sheet, select *Center* to see the picture in the middle of the page *or Tile* to see it repeated to cover your desktop. Click *OK* to finish.

88 CREATE AN ART SCRAPBOOK

You could put together your own art scrapbook with material from the Web. This scrapbook will be a computer document containing a selection of pictures and some information about them.

Choose a picture from the Web.

Insert text and pictures from the Web into a word processing program.

You can find suitable material by searching the Web by key word. To find pictures by a particular artist, use the artist's name and the word "painting", for example **+Monet +painting**. When you find a picture you like, save it as in project 19. To find information about a picture you have saved, search the Web using its title. Save the text you find as in project 56.

Once you have gathered some material, go offline. Start a new document in a word processing program such as *Microsoft®Word*. Copy the pieces of text into this document using the method described in project 56. To add a picture select *Insert* and *Object*. In the window that appears, click on *Create from File*, and then *Browse*. Find one of the pictures you saved, and click on *OK*. The picture, or an icon representing it, will appear in your document. To save your scrapbook, select *Save* from the *File* menu.

89 SEND YOUR OWN PICTURES TO A WEB GALLERY

Try getting your artwork displayed at an online art gallery. There are several galleries on the Web which invite anyone to submit their own artwork for display. One such site is the Children's Art Gallery at **http://redfrog. norconnect.no/~cag/**.

For artwork to appear on the Web, it needs to be saved as a computer document. Artwork on paper can be turned into a computer file by a machine called a scanner (see page 55). This process is called scanning in. If you don't have access to a scanner, companies which develop photographs can often scan in pictures for you.

A scanner divides a picture into tiny dots known as pixels or picture elements. It records information about each pixel and stores all the information it collects as a computer file. You use "imaging" software to tell a scanner how many pixels to divide a picture into. The number of pixels in an image is known as its resolution. It is usually measured in dots per inch (dpi).

Art Web sites usually contain clear instructions for submitting pictures. They normally state what resolution your pictures should be. Most pictures on the Web have a resolution of 75 dpi.

When you have scanned in a picture, use the imaging software to save it as a *GIF* or *JPEG* file. These are the file formats most commonly used for Web images.

The Children's Art Gallery displays artwork by people from all over the world.

Using the Internet is a good way of finding out about things to do, planning days out, and discovering what is going on all over the world. Cameras linked to Net computers allow you to look at some of the places you may want to visit.

90 FIND LOCAL LISTINGS

Newspapers, magazines and Web sites often provide information about activities happening in the near future. Events, such as live music, exhibitions and plays, are grouped together in "listings".

You could use a search engine (see project 3) to find a Web site with listings for the city closest to where you live. Use the name of the city and the word **listings** as key words, for example, **+Glasgow +listings**. On the results pages, click on a link to see a listings site.

Cities and towns all over the world have Web sites that publicize local events.

91 PLAN A SUBWAY JOURNEY

You can plan a subway journey in over 50 different cities throughout the world using the Subway navigator Web site at **http://metro.jussieu.fr:10001/**.

A map of the Paris Metro from Subway navigator

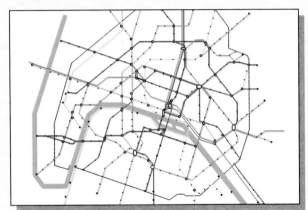

This site helps you to plan a journey between two stations. It tells you the stations your train will stop at and where you need to change trains. For some cities it will even show you your route on a map.

You could, for example, find out how to get from the Gare du Nord station in Paris to Musée du Louvre station, using the Paris Métro. From the Subway navigator home page, click on *Paris*. An online form will appear. Type in **Gare du Nord** next to *Departure station*, and **Musée du Louvre** next to *Arrival station*. Click on *Compute route*. A page will download showing approximately how long the journey will take and the stations you will pass through. To view the route on a map, click on *display*. A map of the Paris Métro will download.

92 SEE LIFE IN A LOCAL STREET

Some towns have set up Web cameras so that people using the Web can have a bird's eye view of what life is like there. (Find out more about Web cameras in project 85.) Sometimes you can see pictures which were taken just a few seconds ago. You can find sites like this by searching the Web using the phrase **"web camera"**.

The English town of Colchester is one town that has a Web camera. You can see its main street. To see a current picture of the street, go to the Actual Size site at **http://www.actual. co.uk/streetcam.html**. You can use your *Reload* button to update the picture.

The Colchester Web camera site

93 LOOK AT A MAP SHOWING YOUR STREET

There are very detailed maps of many major cities on the Web. You can use these to help plan a journey or a day out.

A good place to find maps is the Mapquest Web site at **http://www.mapquest.com/**. To download a map showing a particular street click on *Interactive Atlas (Maps)* on the home page. An online form will appear. Type in the name of a street and its location. For streets outside the USA, you will need to click on the *(or, select country from list)* link. Select the country you require from the list which appears. The country's name will appear in the *Country* box on the online form. Click on the *Search* button to finish.

If Mapquest finds your chosen street, a page will download with one or more small maps. Click on the relevant map to see a larger version.

Maps showing an address in New York

Click on part of the map to enlarge it more.

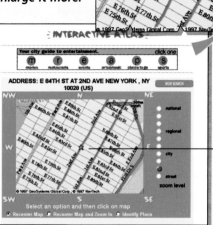

Mapquest can generate local maps for lots of parts of the world.

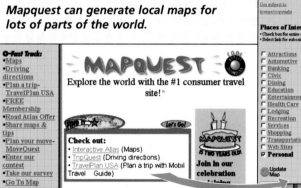

Select Recenter Map and Zoom In, then click on the map to enlarge part of it.

It's surprisingly simple to create your own Web pages. There are two methods you can use. You can either add a code called HTML to a text document to turn it into a Web page, or you can use a program called a Web editor.

Projects 96-101 show you how to create a basic Web page with a Web editor called *Microsoft® FrontPage®Express*. This comes with the browser *Microsoft Internet Explorer 4*, which you can download from **http://www. microsoft.com/**. Start by designing a Web page on your computer. There is information about putting your page on the Web on page 107.

Plan what words and pictures you want to put on your Web page on a piece of paper.

94 VISIT SOME PERSONAL WEB SITES

You can get ideas of things to include on your Web page by looking at other people's sites. People create sites about all kinds of subjects ranging from film stars to soccer. One collection of personal sites is GeoCities, at **http://www.geocities.com/**. To find links to personal sites choose a category, such as *Fashion, Sport* or *Games*, on the home page.

All Web pages and sites are stored on computers called host computers so that Net users can see them. GeoCities provides people with space on host computers free of charge.

Most Internet access providers (see page 55) offer a certain amount of free space for their customers' Web pages.

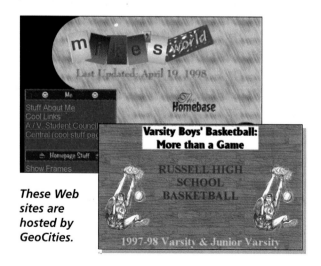

These Web sites are hosted by GeoCities.

95 SET UP A WEB PAGE USING HTML

Try setting up a Web page using HTML. HTML is a set of instructions which tell a browser how to display the information on a Web page. An HTML instruction is called a tag. It appears in brackets like these **< >**.

To set up a very simple page yourself, open a text editing program and create a new document. Type in the codes that appear in brackets exactly as shown below, but you can replace the words outside brackets with your own words. The information that you type in between the two Body tags is the information that will appear on the Web page.

```
<HTML>
<HEAD>
<TITLE>My Page</TITLE>
</HEAD>
<BODY>The text on your page</BODY>
</HTML>
```

Put the title of your page here.

Type in any information you want to include on your Web page here.

Save your page by selecting *Save As* in the *File* menu. Select *Plain text* or *Text document* in the *Save as type* box. Name the file *page.htm*. Save the file into your projects folder (see page 55).

To look at your page, start up your browser. Select *Open, Open File*, or *Open Page* in the *File* menu. Select *page.htm*. Your page will appear. See page 107 for information about transferring a page onto the Web.

96 USE A WEB EDITOR

Web editors are easier to use than HTML (see project 95). You don't need to know any HTML code to create Web pages with a Web editor.

To create a basic page using *FrontPage Express*, start up the program and type some text into the window. You can then use the buttons on the tool bar to add pictures and links, make text larger or smaller, and alter the background of your page.

FrontPage Express always shows the page you're working on as it will appear when seen through a browser. To save your page, select *Save* in the *File* menu. Name the file *web.htm* and save it into your projects folder, as in project 95.

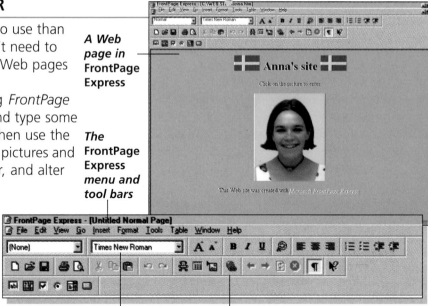

A Web page in FrontPage Express

The FrontPage Express menu and tool bars

Drop-down list of fonts

Use this button to insert a picture.

97 CHANGE THE TEXT STYLE

The text on a Web page must be easy for people to read. You can use different styles and sizes of text to set out the contents of your page clearly. Web text has seven different sizes. Size 1 is the smallest, and size 7 is the largest.

These letters are size 7
This is size 1

This is size 4

You can use these different text sizes on your page.

Enlarge

Reduce

To make a piece of text bigger in *FrontPage Express*, highlight it with your mouse and click once on the *Enlarge* button on the tool bar. This will make it one size larger. To make text smaller, select it and click on the *Reduce* button once.

You can also change the look of your text by making it bold or putting it in italics. To do this, select the text and click on the *Bold*, or the *Italic* button.

B

Bold

Italic

This writing is **bold.**

This piece of writing is in

italics.

Use the bold or italic buttons to get these different styles of text.

You can change the "font" you are using for your text. A font is a distinctive style of lettering. Each style has a different name, for example Times Roman and Helvetica. Try out a few to find one you like. To change the font of a piece of text, highlight it and select a font from the drop-down list on the tool bar.

Examples of different fonts

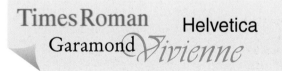

98 CREATE A BACKGROUND

When you create a Web page using *FrontPage Express* (see project 96), it will have a white background. You can make it brighter or more interesting by using a "tiled" background which you create yourself. A tile is a small picture which is repeated to form the background of your page.

Create a tile using a graphics program, for example *Windows 95's Paint*. Open the program and select *Attributes* from the *Image* menu. Specify a canvas size of 3cm by 3cm. Draw an image on your canvas. Keep the image quite pale, so that you will still be able to read the text which will appear on top of the background.

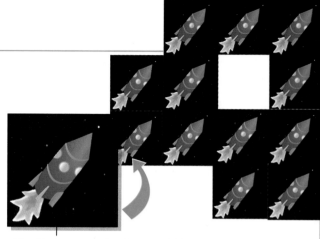

This tile creates a background like this.

This tile creates a fish background.

To save your tile, select *File* and *Save As*. Give it the name *tile.gif* and save it into your *Projects* folder (see page 55).

To use the tile to create a background on your Web page, start *FrontPage Express*, go to the *Format* menu and select *Background*. The *Page Properties* window will appear. On the *Background* sheet, select the *Background Image* box. Click on *Browse* and the *Select Background Image* window will appear. Find *tile.gif*, highlight it and click on *Open*. Click *OK* in the *Page Properties* window.

You will see your tile repeated to form a background on your page.

99 ADD A PHOTOGRAPH

You can use photographs to decorate your Web pages, or as a way of presenting information. For example, you could add a photograph to your Web page to show a sports team you play for, or a band you belong to. To add a photograph to a Web page, you need to start by saving it on your computer. You will need to convert it into a file your computer can use (see project 89).

In *FrontPage Express*, place your cursor where you want to insert the picture on your Web page. Click on the *Add Image* button. In the *Image* box, click on *Browse*. Find the name of your photograph file, and double-click on it.

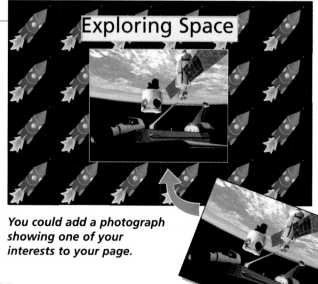

You could add a photograph showing one of your interests to your page.

100 CREATE HYPERLINKS

The links on Web pages are called hyperlinks. You can create hyperlinks to join your Web page to other sites. Visitors to your site can follow hyperlinks to find out more about a subject. For example, if your page includes some information about the pop star Madonna, you could create a link to a site belonging to her record company or a page where you can hear one of her songs.

In *FrontPage Express*, choose a word, phrase, or picture to turn into a link, and highlight it using your mouse. Click on the *Link* tool on your button bar. The *Create Hyperlink* box will appear. In the <u>URL:</u> box, type the URL of the page you are linking to. Click on *OK*.

Barbara **also has a web page**

A hyperlink

The piece of text or picture you choose will be turned into a hyperlink. A text link will turn blue, and it will be underlined. A picture link will not look any different on your screen in *FrontPage Express* but some browsers may place a border around it. You can tell if a picture on a Web page is a hyperlink by passing your mouse over it. If a picture is a hyperlink your mouse pointer will turn into a hand pointer.

101 SAY HELLO TO VISITORS

It's possible to add a sound clip to your Web page so that it plays automatically when someone downloads your page. To record a sound you will need to use a microphone, and a sound recording program such as *Sound Recorder*, which is provided with *Windows 95*.

Say, for example, you want to include a greeting. Start up *Sound Recorder*, click on the *Record* button, and say "hello" into your microphone. Then click on the *Stop* button.

You have now created a sound file. Select *Save <u>A</u>s* from the *<u>F</u>ile* menu to save it, and name it *hello.wav*. Once you've saved your sound file, you can click on the *Play* button to hear it replayed.

The Sound Recorder window

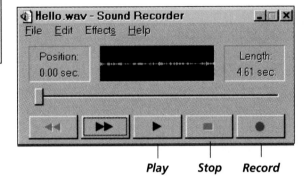

Play   Stop   Record

To add the sound to your page, go to the *<u>I</u>nsert* menu in *FrontPage Express* and select *Backgrou<u>n</u>d Sound*. Use the *Browse* window to select your sound's filename. Your page won't look any different, but when someone downloads it they will hear you saying hello.

PUTTING YOUR PAGE ON THE WEB

When you have completed your Web page you can put it on the Web. This is called uploading. After you upload your page, anyone surfing the Web will be able to see it.

The exact uploading method will vary depending on who is hosting the page (see project 94). To get full instructions look at your host's Web site, or call their helpline.

The Internet brings the world to your computer. This means that you might come across things you don't like. Follow the guidelines on this page, and throughout the book, to stay safe as you use the Internet.

 A computer virus is a program which attacks your computer's memory and can cause it permanent damage. When using the Net, it's possible to download a computer virus with another program by accident. Use a virus checker program on all the files you download before you open them. You can get an evaluation version of a virus checker from **http://www.drsolomon.com/**. Regularly check your entire C drive for viruses. (Many experts suggest that you should do this once a week.)

 If you receive an e-mail containing anything you don't like, delete it immediately.

 If you find anything on the Web which makes you feel upset or uncomfortable, use your browser's *Stop* button, and visit another page instead.

 Never arrange to meet someone in person whom you've only met on the Internet.

 Don't give your full name, address or telephone number, to someone you have only met on the Net. Remember that the people you meet there are strangers and may not be who they say they are.

USING FILTERS

There are a number of programs which you can install on your computer that will prevent it downloading unpleasant material. These programs are called filters, and they work by blocking access to certain types of material on the Internet. You can download them from their Web sites.

Some of the most popular Web filters and their URLs

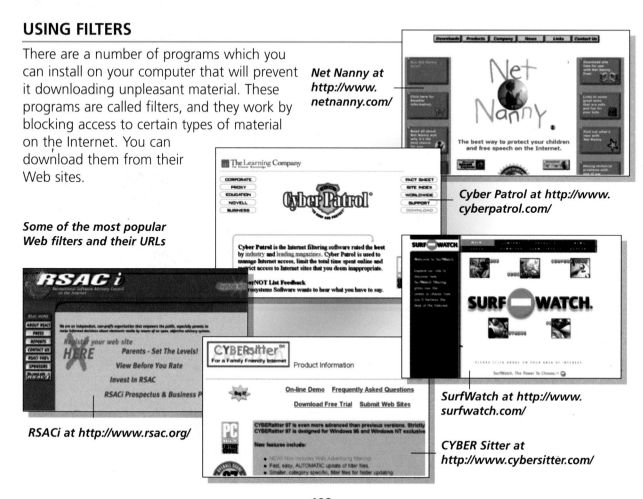

Net Nanny at http://www.netnanny.com/

Cyber Patrol at http://www.cyberpatrol.com/

RSACi at http://www.rsac.org/

SurfWatch at http://www.surfwatch.com/

CYBER Sitter at http://www.cybersitter.com/

ACKNOWLEDGMENTS

Usborne Publishing Ltd. has taken every care to ensure that the instructions contained in this book are accurate and suitable for their intended purpose. However, they are not responsible for the content of, and do not sponsor, any Web site not owned by them, including those listed below, nor are they responsible for any exposure to offensive or inaccurate material which may appear on the Web.

Microsoft®Windows®95, Microsoft®Internet Explorer, Microsoft®Word and Microsoft®FrontPage®Express are either registered trademarks or trademarks of Microsoft Corporation in the United States and other countries. Netscape, Netscape Navigator, and the N logo are registered trademarks of Netscape Communications Corporation in the United States and other countries. Netscape Messenger, Netscape Communicator, Collabra, and Netcaster are also trademarks of Netscape Communications Corporation, which may be registered in other countries.
Java and all Java-based trademarks and logos are trademarks or registered trademarks of Sun Microsystems, Inc. in the United States and other countries.

Photographs
p.50 Optical disk: Telegraph Colour Library (also p.92).
p.51 Biker: Empics (also p.69); p.53 Videoconferencing images courtesy of Intel®Corp (also p.91); p.54 Computer courtesy of Apple Computers; Accura 288 Message Modem supplied by Hayes Microcomputer Products, Inc.; HP Netserver E50 courtesy of Hewlett-Packard Ltd.; Earth from space: European Space Agency/Science Photo Library.
p.55 Microphone courtesy of Creative Labs (also p.90). HP Deskjet 820CXi printer courtesy of Hewlett-Packard Ltd. Connectix QuickCam VC used courtesy of Connectix Corporation; Scanner courtesy of Epson Ltd.; p.66 Dolphin photo: David Hofmann; p.67 Macaws: Tony Stone Images.
p.68 Tennis Player: SuperStock Ltd (also p.49); Tennis ball: SuperStock Ltd (also p.49); Snowboarder: SuperStock Ltd. American footballer: The Stock Market Photo Agency UK. pp.70-71 Musical instruments: Howard Allman; p.73 Hong Kong: The Stock Market Photo Agency UK; p.82 Statue: The Stock Market Photo Agency UK (also p.49); Writing montage: SuperStock Ltd (also p.49); Prayer Book: Tony Stone Images (also p.49); p.83 Computer: SuperStock Ltd.
Pile of books: The Stock Market Photo Agency UK; p.87 Food: Howard Allman; p.90 Speakers courtesy of Creative Labs; p.92 Money: Telegraph Colour Library; Gift, t-shirt, flowers: Ray Moller, Amanda Heywood, Sue Atkinson; p.96 UFO: The Stock Market Photo Agency UK; p.97 Alien art: Gary Bines; p.101 Painting: Vanessa Wilson.

Screen shots
p.52 German government site used with permission.
http://www.bundesregierung.de/
p.53 CU-SeeMe is a registered trademark of White Pine Software, http://www.wpine.com/ (also p.91).
Avatars courtesy of Onlive, Inc. (also p.91, with screen shot).
p.56 Screen shot reprinted by permission from Microsoft Corporation.
With thanks to the White House.
p.57 AltaVista reproduced with the permission of Digital Equipment Corporation. AltaVista and the AltaVista logo are trademarks of Digital Equipment Corporation (also pages 59 and 95).
Excite, WebCrawler, the Excite logo and the Webcrawler logo are trademarks of Excite, Inc. and may be registered in various jurisdictions. Excite screen display copyright 1995-1997 Excite, Inc.
Hotbot copyright © 1994-97 HotWired, Inc. All rights reserved.
Infoseek logo reprinted by permission. Infoseek and the Infoseek logo are trademarks of Infoseek Corporation which may be registered in certain jurisdictions. Other trademarks shown are trademarks of their respective owners. Copyright © 1994-1998 Infoseek Corporation. All rights reserved.
Yahoo! text and artwork copyright © 1997 by Yahoo! Inc. all rights reserved. Yahoo! and the Yahoo! logo are trademarks of Yahoo! Inc. (also pages 58, 59, 78 and 85).
Magellan Internet Guide and the Magellan logo are trademarks of The McKinley Group, Inc., a subsidiary of Excite, Inc., and may be registered in various jurisdictions. Magellan screen display copyright 1998 of The McKinley Group, Inc., a subsidiary of Excite, Inc.
Lycos logo copyright © 1994-97 Carnegie Mellon University. All rights reserved. Lycos is a registered trademark of Carnegie Mellon University. Used by permission.
The Chimpanzee Zone **http://www.lancs.ac.uk/ staff/mckee/chimp.html** used with permission.
p.59 Rugrats © 1998 Viacom International Inc. All rights reserved. Rugrats and all related titles, logos and characters are trademarks of Viacom International Inc. Created by Klasy-Csupo, Inc.
p.60 Netscape Messenger and Collabra screens copyright 1998 Netscape Communications Corp. Used with permission. All rights reserved. This electronic file or page may not be copied without the express written permission of Netscape (also page 70).
p.61 Activegrams site used with permission.
http://www.activegrams.com/
p.62 RealPlayer™ is either a registered trademark or trademark of RealNetworks, Inc. in the United States and/or other countries (also page 71).
p.63 WinZip copyright 1991-1997, Nico Mak Computing, Inc. Printed with permission of Nico Mak Computing, Inc.
p.64 With thanks to NASA (also page 51).
p.65 Hubble image: material that appears in this book was created with support to Space Telescope Science Institute, operated by the Association of Universities for Research in Astronomy, Inc., from NASA contract NAS5-26555, and is reproduced here with permission from AURA/STScI. Photos: J. Hester and P. Scowen (Arizona State Univ.), and NASA. Ask An Astronaut pages reproduced with permission of the National Space Society.
p.66 Hummingbird photo: David Roles; Bamboo: R.D.E. MacPhee (American Museum of Natural History); Pandas, tigers: courtesy Department of Library Services, American Museum of Natural History; Acmepet logo reproduced with permission.
http://www.acmepet.com/
p.67 National Wildlife Federation screen shot reproduced from the Web site of the National Wildlife Federation (**http://www.nwf.org/**) with the permission of its creator and publisher, the National Wildlife Federation. Copyright © 1997 by the National Wildlife Federation.
Treasured Earth HTML page by Rod Borland.
http://www.ten.org/
WWF-UK page © WWF-UK.
p.68 Sydney 2000 screen shot: copyrights and TM rights of this page are SOCOG owned.
Olympique Lyonnais images reproduced with permission.
http://www.olympiquelyonnais.com/
p.69 Liszt home page reproduced with permission.
http://www.liszt.com/
Chelsea images copyright Chelsea Communications, **http://www.chelseafc.co.uk/**, and Active Images.
p.71 Virgin Radio, the UK's favourite radio station. Listen now in stereo: **http://www.virginradio.co.uk/**
p.72 The Mad Scientist Network, Washington University School of Medicine.
StudyWeb site used with permission.
http://www.studyweb.com/
Homework Help site used with permission.

http://www.startribune.com/homework/
p.73 travlang screen shots courtesy of travlang, http://www.travlang.com/, copyright 1998 travlang and Michael C Martin; Research It! by iTools!
http://www.iTools.com/research-it/
Biographical Dictionary used with permission.
http://www.s9.com/biography/
p.74 Spaceship picture courtesy of Virgin Interactive Entertainment; Virtual Pool 2 courtesy of Interplay Productions Limited; Sim City 2000 courtesy of Maxis; Monopoly courtesy of Hasbro Interactive.
p.75 Magic: The Gathering © 1997 Wizards of the Coast, Inc. Magic: The Gathering and Wizards of the Coast are registered trademarks of Wizards of the Coast. MicroProse Software, Inc. is an official licensee. MicroProse is a registered trademark of MicroProse Software, Inc. Computer code © 1997 MicroProse Software, Inc. All rights reserved.
Ultimate Race Pro © 1996/1998 Kalisto Technologies. All rights reserved. Ultimate Race Pro and Kalisto Entertainment are trademarks of Kalisto Technologies. Microprose is a registered trademark of Microprose Ltd.
p.76 Men In Black © 1998 Columbia Tristar Interactive. All rights reserved; Space Jam/Warner Bros. courtesy Warner Bros. Online. Interactive Simulation courtesy of 'The Motion-Picture Industry: Behind-the-Scenes' Web site. Used by permission.
p.77 Independence Day site used with permission.
http://www.id4movie.com/
Internet Movie Database icon used with permission.
http://www.imdb.com/
p.78 One Sky, Many Voices site used with permission.
http://onesky.engin.umich.edu/
Weather photos: lightning/clouds: Michael Bath, sunrise/ aerial clouds: Jimmy Deguara, dust devil: John Roenfeldt.
p.79 WinWeather used with permission.
http://www.igsnet.com
p.80 Dinosaur pictures: Joe Tucciarone.
Hunterian Museum site used with permission.
http://www.gla.ac.uk/Museum/
p.81 DinoShred screen saver © Fiore Industries Inc., Albuquerque, NM, USA.
p.82 OKUKBooks home page reproduced with permission.
http://www.okukbooks.com/
Amazon.com home page reproduced with permission (also p.92). http://www.amazon.com/
barnesandnoble.com home page reproduced with permission.
http://www.barnesandnoble.com/
p.83 KidPub home page/logo copyright 1998 KidPub Worldwide Publishing, used by permission.
Internet Public Library home page reproduced with permission.
http://www.ipl.org/
p.84 Screen grab from BBC Online Channel reproduced by kind permission of the BBC.
Le Monde site used with permission. http://www.lemonde.fr/
USA Today site copyright 1997 USA Today.
Copyright The Press On-Line, http://www.press.co.nz
a division of The Christchurch Press Co Ltd, Pvt Bag, Christchurch, NZ.
Kidlink site used with permission. http://www.kidlink.org/
p.85 Crayon site copyright 1998, NetPressence, Inc.
p.86 Gourmet World copyright © 1998 International Web Broadcasting Corporation; Pizza Online site used with permission. http://www.pizzaonline.com/
p.87 Internet Pizza Server image used with permission.
http://www.ecst.csuchico.edu/~pizza
p.88 Swiss Photogallery site used with permission.
http://therion.minpet.unibas.ch/minpet/gallery/
Land of Beauty site used with permission.
http://www.cnd.org/Scenery/
Jamaica site used with permission.
http://www.jamaicatravel.com/

E-Cards site courtesy of the E-Cards Team. http://www.e-cards.com/
p.89 Tidal Passages is a project managed and developed by WinStar for Education http://www.win4edu.com and Lorna Metzger lorna@tidalpassages.com
RoadTripAmerica site used with permission.
http://www.roadtripamerica.com
p.90 mIRC copyright © 1998 mIRC Co. Ltd.
p.91 Active Worlds used with permission.
http://www.activeworlds.com/
p.92 Toys"R"Us site courtesy of Toys"R"Us.
HMV site used with permission. http://www.hmv.co.uk/
p.93 eCash purse courtesy of DigiCash Inc., copyright DigiCash Inc., 1994-1998. All rights reserved. http://www.digicash.com/
Barbie is a trademark owned and used with permission of Mattel, Inc. © 1998 Mattel, Inc. All rights reserved.
Reebok.com/Reebok International Ltd. used with permission.
p.94 Lung icon courtesy of South Coast Air Quality Management District, Diamond Bar, CA; Panorama: Eric Goetze (erik@outre.com). Recycle City site used with thanks to the United States Environmental Protection Agency.
p.95 Greenpeace International site used with permission.
http://www.greenpeace.org/
Greenpeace UK site courtesy of Greenpeace at Knowhaus Ltd. Greenpeace Argentina site © Gunnberg/ w3Comunicacioñ.
http://w3.com.ar
p.96 ISUR picture used with permission. http://www.isur.com/
Fortean Times is copyright John Brown Publishing/ Fortean Times. No associated images may be reproduced without permission.
Crop Circle pictures: Freddy Silva.
p.97 Animated Alien Cursors created by Eileen Fitzgibbons of Orlando, Florida, US. http://www. parkave.net/users/fitz/ fitz@parkave.net
GhostWatcher site courtesy of June Houston.
http://www.flyvision.org/sitelite/Houston/ GhostWatcher/
GhostWeb at http://www.ghostweb.com is the official Web site of the International Ghost Hunters Society.
p.98 Kobe pictures © City of Kobe. All rights reserved.
p.99 USGS images courtesy of USGS/Cascades Volcano Observatory.
p.100 Exploratorium images © 1998 The Exploratorium, reproduced with permission.
p.101 The Children's Art Gallery site used with permission.
http://redfrog.norconnect.no/~cag/
p.102 Vivi Cagliari by Sardegna On Line Magazine, http://www.sardegna.com/ by Asanet SRL.
Cape Town site used with permission. http://www.ctcc.gov.za/
Manukau site used with permission.
http://www.manukau.govt.nz/
Subway Navigator created by Pierre David.
p.103 Colchester Web camera image used with permission.
http://www.actual.co.uk/
Mapquest maps (www.mapquest.com) copyright GeoSystems Global Corp.
p.104 Mike's World site used with permission, created by Michael Jutan, a high school student from London, Ontario, Canada.
http://www.geocities.com/TimesSquare/2211/
Russell High School Basketball site used with permission.
http://www.geocities.com/Colosseum/Arena/8156/
p.105 Photo courtesy of Anna Milbourne.
p.108 Net Nanny site used with permission.
http://www.netnanny.com/
CyberPatrol © 1998 The Learning Company, Inc.
Surfwatch, the pioneer of, and leader in, Internet filtering software.
RSACi site copyright 1998 RSACi, used with permission.
http://www.rsac.org/
CYBERsitter site used with permission.
http://www.cybersitter.com/